The Cowboy's Sweet Elopement

THE COWBOY'S SWEET ELOPEMENT

THE COWBOYS OF SWEETHEART CREEK, TEXAS
BOOK 4

JEAN ORAM

The Cowboy's Sweet Elopement
The Cowboys of Sweetheart Creek, Texas Book 4

By Jean Oram

© 2021 Jean Oram
First edition
All rights reserved

Printed in the United States of America unless otherwise stated on the last page of this book. Published by Oram Productions Alberta, Canada.

COMPLETE LIBRARY OF CONGRESS CATALOGING-IN-PUBLICATION DATA AVAILABLE ONLINE

Oram, Jean.

The Cowboy's Sweet Elopement / Jean Oram.—1st. ed.

ISBN: 978-1-989359-35-8, 978-1-989359-36-5

Ebook ISBN: 978-1-989359-37-2

First Oram Productions Edition: January 2021

Cover design by Jean Oram

When you write a book you never know when and where real life and fiction will converge.

When a friend will tease you and accidentally name the ranch of your new series.

When your own washing machine will kick the bucket (slowly and in the most agonizing way over a period of months) and your own real life hero will buy you a new one while you work on finishing up a book. But honestly… why is the machine *MINE* anyway?

You also never know when going to a county water wellness workshop for well owners will give you a small slice to add to a story—such as Tadpole. (Animals do sometimes get caught in well pits, and Brant's quest to have them banned is a real thing.)

I hope you enjoy the slices of real life merged with fiction, and that Brant and April's story sweeps you up in the most magical way.

With love,
Jean Oram
Alberta, Canada 2020

ACKNOWLEDGMENTS

I'd like to thank Nathan for naming Tadpole for me. With the shutdown of schools during COVID-19, the 2020 autumn edition, I'd often turn to him where he was sitting at his own desk beside mine and ask him for a character name. Tadpole was the perfect name (and very Brantlike) for the kitten found in the well pit.

I'd also like to thank my real life hero for arranging to have our piece of crap washing machine hauled away while I worked on edits for this book. I got so much more done while writing when I no longer had to sprint up to the main floor to stop the washing machine from refilling with water again and again while I fought with it to spin our clothes. Although, come to think of it, what are the kids and I going to do in the evenings if we aren't standing in the laundry room, babysitting the machine while watching Netflix on my iPad? (I'm sure we'll think of something.)

A heartfelt thanks goes to Margaret Carney and Tessa Shapcott for their edits and suggestions. I'd also like to thank my beta team: Margaret C., Sharon S., Donna W., Erika H., and Lucy J. for making sure I didn't forget to mention things like where on earth the scenes were actually taking place. And finally, to my HEAs for their last minute catches—thank you!

"Where's the gift for Brant?" April MacFarlane asked her four-year-old son, as she sifted through the torn wrapping paper under the small tree by the front window. It was a slim blue package, and she feared it might have gotten shredded or lost in the Christmas-morning mess.

Kurt beamed up at her, his face smeared with the chocolate he'd eaten from his Christmas stocking. He'd barely stopped moving since six that morning, his belief in Santa and everything good still strong despite the recent divorce of his parents. Christmas was truly magical.

Even Heath, Kurt's father, had paused his battle with her long enough to get their son a gift—though he hadn't yet arrived for a quick morning hello as promised, and it was nearly noon.

"Here it is," April exclaimed, pulling the wrinkled package out from under a yellow tractor. She smoothed the wrapping paper, knowing her son had worked hard on this gift for their family friend Brant Wylder, who was due to pop by shortly.

Kurt bounced his way across the couch and snagged it from her hands. "I want to give it to Daddy Brant."

"Daddy Brant?" she repeated, her body stilling.

It was true the two of them had spent more time around Brant lately, and that her son looked up to him. But there was no reason for him to grant the sweetheart of a man daddy status. Even though there had been the odd heated look passing between her and Brant lately.

But he wasn't about to be Kurt's new daddy anytime soon. Brant had a habit of rescuing women like the strays that came into his veterinarian clinic, and sadly, that was April's current status. So if he did make a move, it would likely be borne out of his need to save her. It wouldn't be because he saw her as a sexy and appealing woman he wanted to date.

But that's what New Year's resolutions were for. Even though the holiday was a week away, April had already made hers. She was going to straighten out her life, and prove to herself and the community that she had become more than the impetuous gal Brant had grown up alongside on the ranch. More than some female who cried on his shoulder when life and her whirlwind romances didn't turn out like her fantasies. More than a woman down on her luck and in need of a hand up.

"When's he gonna get here?" Kurt asked, bouncing across the cushions again.

April picked him up and set him on the floor. "No jumping on the couch. And you can't call Brant 'Daddy.' He's just a friend."

"Colby got a new daddy. Why can't I?"

"You have one," April said firmly. Heath just didn't act like a dad very often. Partly because his job as a rodeo stock contractor kept him on the road a lot, and partly because he hadn't been quite ready to be a father. Or a husband.

"I never see Daddy," Kurt whined.

April sighed, and whispered, "I know, sweetie."

"Why can't Brant be my daddy?" Kurt asked with a stubborn pout.

"It doesn't work that way." Although she had to admit the man would make an amazing father. He'd been the one to teach Kurt how to tie his shoelaces and had been there when he'd counted to ten for the first time, last week. He was sweet, kind, and made both her and Kurt happy.

"Brant's just a friend," April repeated, her heart sinking as she admitted that truth.

"Is he a firefighter?"

"What? No. He's a veterinarian and a rancher. You know that." Kurt spent time on the Sweet Meadows Ranch as well as at Brant's clinic, Call of the Wyld(er), where she worked as a part-time receptionist.

"Mrs. Fisher said Daddy Brant is good at rescuing you."

April rocked back on her heels. All the more reason to get her life on track again if even the gossips at the diner saw her in the same way she feared Brant did, and were talking about it in front of her son.

"He's a helpful friend," April said patiently. "You ignore what you hear from others, okay? And you need to call him Brant, sweetie. Not Daddy Brant."

She could only imagine the gossip that would start if that name got out. Brant had been instrumental in helping her leave her marriage to Heath just before Christmas, and some people were already speculating about her and Brant, even though she'd spent two years on her own working up the courage to quit.

"Now go wash your face. He'll be here soon."

Kurt ran around the couch, making revving sounds. "I hope he gets here right now!"

"Wash your face."

Her son spun off into the bathroom, but when the doorbell rang moments later, he ran out again, dripping chocolaty water.

"Dry your face!" April said, watching the drops hit the floor. "But wash better first, okay?"

Kurt pivoted sharply, returning to his task. April took a moment to smooth her red sweater before heading to the door. One hand on the knob, she inhaled, then exhaled, calming the butterflies in her stomach. When she and Brant were teenagers, he'd been a strong, dependable friend, and nothing more.

But somewhere along the line things had changed for her. Somewhere between all the tears Brant had dried when she'd whirlwind dated his older brother Cole, breaking up so many times and making up again during their early twenties that April had lost count. Somewhere between then and finding out she was pregnant, after what was supposed to be a rebound relationship with Heath Thompson. Or maybe it had changed more recently, when she'd walked away from her marriage to rebuild her life, and had found Brant there, hand extended, ready to help.

He had always been there for her, encouraging her to laugh, supporting her decisions, making her now-generous curves feel downright sexy despite how tightly her clothes fit. But she'd only recently realized that he was exactly what she'd always been looking for. And that he was returning her lingering gazes.

All she had to do was straighten out her life and be a strong, self-sufficient woman who could stand as an equal in front of him, ready to offer her heart.

With one last inhale to battle the butterflies, April opened the door, unable to hide her cheerful smile at seeing a handsome Brant Wylder on her doorstep.

***

BRANT STRAIGHTENED his collar as he waited for April to open the door. She had hung the wreath she'd made with his mother and his brothers' girlfriends, Laura Oakes, Karen Hartley and Carly Clarke, plus family friend Jackie Moorhouse. They'd collected boughs and pinecones out on the ranch's back forty last week, then taken over the kitchen table to hot glue it all together into festive wreaths. Hers swung outward on its hook as the door opened, before thumping back into place.

April, in a V-necked woolly sweater that hugged her curves,

looked as irresistible as always. Then again, he figured she could be in pajama pants and a sweatshirt, her hair in a sloppy ponytail, and he would still think she was the prettiest woman in all of Sweetheart Creek.

He'd always thought that, but growing up beside each other and being her confidant, he'd found himself solidly in the friend zone. It hadn't helped that she'd been seduced by adventure and the need to get noticed by her ranch-hand father, who'd been more than happy to let Maria and Roy Wylder, Brant's parents, do the upbringing while he kept their cattle in line.

Sometimes Brant wondered whether he'd have caught April's eye in their teens if he'd been more like his brother Cole, more determined to stand out from the Wylder pack. He had a feeling the timing wouldn't have been right, and that it would never have worked.

But now…

Now things were different. *They* were different.

There was a strength and heat building between them that hadn't been there before. They had a solid friendship to build on, and while he knew it was early for her to be thinking about another romance, he wanted to be part of her life and her family. He wanted her to rely on him, wanted to be the one she kissed at night. He wanted to be the man she woke up next to each morning.

He just needed to be patient.

Today her smile was shy, but not so much he didn't see the hint of her dimples or the sparkle in her glance as she ushered him into her home. He lifted his cowboy hat with a nod and a "Ma'am" that caused her to roll her eyes and give him a playful swat.

He grinned, and she smiled back, even though he knew she didn't want to reward his "ma'am" behavior. That quick forgiveness told him there was definitely something brewing between them, and that it wasn't one-sided.

Not at all.

Especially when her slow gaze drank him in from boots to belt buckle and on up to his carefully chosen hat.

"Daddy Brant!" Kurt called, ripping around the corner, a wrapped gift clutched in his hands. His eyes were wide with joy, his face red as if he'd just given it a good scrubbing. His words swelled Brant's heart to a dangerous size. Was there anything he wouldn't do for this kid?

Or his mother?

April gave Kurt a warning look as he slid to a stop in front of Brant in his blue-and-red firetruck pajamas.

"Just Brant," she said firmly.

"Just Brant," he said solemnly, causing Brant to chuckle. "I made you this. It's a present."

He ruffled Kurt's brown hair and shot April a questioning look. What was with the Daddy Brant thing? He sure didn't mind, but he also knew it wouldn't help the rumors floating around town that she'd left Heath in order to be with him.

Yes, the two of them were close. Yes, they'd spent a lot more time together lately. But so far nothing had happened other than him saving her from a loveless marriage by setting her up with a home and a job so she could take care of her son while starting over.

Brant was still in the friend zone. And if the town couldn't see that, then he doubted there was much he could do about it.

"What do we have here?" he asked, turning over the floppy gift. There was a lot of jaggedly cut wrapping paper and plenty of tape. "Is this from you?"

Kurt's breath quickened as he nodded. "Open it!"

"Why don't you come in and take your coat off?" April gestured to the living room. Brant had made it about three feet into the house, just far enough to close the door behind him.

"I think I'd better open this first," he said seriously, and she gave him a soft look that made his swelling heart expand once again.

Kurt reached up. "I'll help you!"

"Kurt," she warned, "it's Brant's gift."

Her son's excitement dampened, and he put his hands behind his back.

"What is it?" Brant asked, slowly peeling away the layers of wrapping to reveal a piece of water-wrinkled computer paper. He turned it over to see a bright painting.

"It's a picture! I painted it. It's of you. See all the animals?" Kurt crowded close, pointing at various swatches of color.

Brant pulled the rest of the wrap away. "Well, look at that. It is me. And a lot of animals. I must be at work."

"You are. You just undeaded that cow. And this one had babies. And this kitten is the one you saved from a burning barn. See the barn over here? It's on fire." There was a swath of red and orange in the corner.

Brant smiled at the heroic version of himself. "Wow. There's a lot going on in this painting. Thank you, Kurt."

"You can put it on your fridge."

"Thank you. I will." He held it up to admire it further. "Which fridge? The one at the ranch or the one in my veterinarian clinic?"

Kurt thought that over, and Brant took a second to glance at April. She was smiling again, her bottom lip pulled between her teeth. And looking from him to Kurt with so much love, he had a feeling he'd made her morning, just by showing her son the affection he deserved.

Hopefully, she'd soon be ready to allow him to do the same for her.

"I have something for you, too," April said, as Brant stepped into the living room.

"They're coupons!" Kurt said. "But you don't have to spend any money to use them."

April shot him a warning frown. "It's not fair to spoil someone else's gift."

"That's okay," Brant said smoothly. "I still don't know what the coupons are for, right?"

April retrieved the tiny gift bag from under the Christmas tree while Kurt and Brant settled on the couch. She had borrowed Karen Hartley's scrapbooking equipment and poured hours into making the pretty coupons, wanting them to feel like a real gift worth giving rather than something she'd made, that cost nothing.

She took the empty spot beside Brant, not minding how the old couch tipped her closer to him.

He opened the Christmas-themed bag and looked inside, then pulled out the handful of coupons. His eyebrows lifted in surprise. "Wow. I didn't know you scrapbook."

"Karen taught me."

Brant's eyes, blue as the sky, met hers and she immediately understood that he knew how much time and care she'd put into the gift, cutting the tiny letters, pasting them onto layers of decorative paper.

"Thank you," he said softly, still looking at her. His eyes trailed to her lips, and she had a fleeting thought that she should have made a coupon for a free kiss.

"You have to read them now," Kurt demanded from Brant's other side, jostling him.

"No, you don't," April said, suddenly feeling shy.

Brant obliged Kurt by thumbing through them, murmuring under his breath. "Help with ranch chores, free home-cooked meal, one cowboy boot cleaning including oil or lotion, one batch of homemade cookies, one pretend-you're-not-at-work diversion from the reception desk... I'm using that one!" He continued through them, carefully tucking them back into the gift bag when he was done. "These are amazing. Thank you."

"You should get my mom to make you spaghetti," Kurt said, leaving the couch to face Brant. "It's my favorite, but don't put Parmesan on top because it's stinky."

Brant chuckled. "Thanks for the tip."

"You are welcome, sir," Kurt said crisply. "Do you have a gift for me?"

"Kurt!" April said. "That's rude."

But all three of them knew he did, as even on ordinary days he seemed to have a little something. When she'd been married, Brant would pop in when a work call brought him out her way, often with a little trinket for her or Kurt. Sometimes it was an apple fritter, if he'd passed by Maples in Riverbend. Sometimes it was a dinosaur-shaped rock, or one time a cow's tooth, which had delighted Kurt to no end. They were small things, but showed Brant was thinking of them, and it made her feel special in the quiet, everyday moments. And different from how anyone else had ever made her feel.

"As a matter fact, I do have something," he told Kurt.

"I knew it! What is it? What is it?" Kurt asked, jumping up and down.

"It's in my truck."

"Is it a dog? A puppy? I really wanna dog." Kurt ran to the door.

April inhaled through her teeth, sending Brant a look of desperation. She really wanted a dog, too, but wasn't quite prepared.

"Sorry, I can't just show up with an animal," Brant said, holding the door for Kurt, who hadn't even paused to pull on boots. "A dog is a serious commitment and costs a lot of money."

"You can do it for us," Kurt said, rushing down the sidewalk.

"We have to take care of our own things!" April called after him, a renewed resolution to become more self-sufficient reviving inside her. When she was around Brant it was all too easy to let his naturally caring side kick in, allowing him to do more than he truly should. And apparently Kurt saw it, too.

Brant put an arm around her, pulling her against him in the doorway for a mini hug. As though reading her thoughts, he said, "Give yourself time."

"I hate worrying about money. It makes me feel…" She shook her hands as if ready to throttle the feeling that had clawed up inside her, and he dropped his arm. When he opened his mouth, she was pretty sure he was going to say she could stay here in his house, rent-free, for as long as she wanted. After all, he'd bought it from his brother's girlfriend solely for the purpose of letting her live here, before eventually turning it into a rental property.

"I know," she went on, before he could speak. "And I am immensely grateful. But I also need to show my son that I can stand on my own two feet."

Brant nodded. "I understand." There was a renewed respect in his gaze.

"What is it? Is it a horse?" Kurt was shouting from beside Brant's truck, which had the ranch's horse trailer hooked up behind it. "Am I joining the rodeo?"

"You said no animals, right?" April confirmed as they went to catch up with Kurt. Brant just grinned at her before opening the doors to the trailer.

"Whoa!" Kurt scrambled inside as she leaned into take a better look.

"A playhouse?" It had shingles on the roof, an open door and window, a little front porch with an overhang, and it was big enough to hold a few children. Which of course made her think about making some with Brant.

"A fort," both Brant and Kurt corrected at the same time.

"For playing cowboys and bad guys," Brant called into the

trailer. "You can make it a jail, or a stable, or whatever your imagination wants."

"Cool!" Kurt said from inside the playhouse.

Her coupons felt so small compared to this amazing gift. "This is huge."

"Nah. Myles and I made it in a day." Brant gave her a cheerful smile, and she could tell he was delighted to be giving Kurt something that was bringing him so much joy. "We started a few days ago, when he was still mad at Ryan over the State football game decisions and had all that energy to burn. We just sort of began with what we found in the equipment shed, and by the end of the day this is what we had."

"It's amazing."

"Mom, can I bring my new tractor in here to play?" Kurt asked.

"I was thinking we could put this in the backyard," Brant said.

"Yeah!" Her son came blasting out. "Do you have the truck keys?"

Brant chuckled and held them out of Kurt's reach. "I'll drive. And we're going to need some help, as it's pretty heavy. I'll text my brothers, okay?"

Kurt disappeared back inside the fort.

Before long three Wylder brothers, Myles, Levi and Ryan, were working together with Brant to get the new playhouse into the backyard. Then, just as quickly as they'd arrived, they were off again, with a promise to see them all at the ranch for Christmas dinner.

Kurt was still outside playing in the new fort in his pajamas, and April took him his jacket before sitting on the back step with Brant. The day was cool, and they draped a blanket across their shoulders, enjoying the peacefulness with cups of coffee.

Times like this she could envision what it would feel like to have her life together again, to be ready to pursue something special with Brant, to savor quiet moments in the day together.

"I think he's going to want to sleep out here," April said, watching Kurt play, his lively imagination at work.

"Sorry." Brant winced, but didn't look at all apologetic.

She laughed. "You're not."

"True."

Her phone buzzed, and she checked to see if it was her dad calling to say Merry Christmas. Her mom, living in Dallas, had called earlier from a vacation she was taking in Europe. But so far her father hadn't replied to her voice mail. Her screen showed a text message from Heath. She skimmed it, not wanting to interrupt this moment with Brant.

"What's wrong?" he asked, his forehead creasing.

"Nothing." April set her phone facedown on the step beside her. She was tempted to pour her grievances out to Brant, as per her habit, but it was time to stop treating him like her dumping ground, leaving her problems for him to fix.

Besides, Heath's reply to her reminder text that Kurt expected to see him today would anger Brant the same way it had angered her. Heath had replied, saying he would pop by if she agreed to go on a date with him.

They were divorced! What was he thinking? He'd signed the papers almost immediately when he'd received them. There had been no hassle at all until they got to custody and support payments. He felt he shouldn't have to pay a dime. April felt otherwise, having spent the past several years doing the books for his company, living in his house, and building up nothing of her own.

Since the day she'd first talked about separating, two years ago, Heath had been erratic. One moment it appeared he wanted her gone, the next he was pulling stuff like this as though afraid to let her go. They'd argued and fought, then vowed to try harder. It never worked. And now here they were, at what should be the simple part, and he was playing games. She didn't like it. Especially since some of them involved their son.

"Heath?" Brant asked.

She grimaced. "So is there anything I need to do with the playhouse?" It had been painted and finished, though it was missing a door and a glass window. Both items had likely been left off intentionally. "Upkeep-wise?"

"He didn't show up this morning, did he?" Brant said, not accepting her topic change.

April felt her shoulders droop. She was tired of the sympathy in his kind gaze. Every time Heath messed up it brought out the protective side in Brant. She adored it, but it embarrassed her that people were calling his helpfulness for what it truly was—a rescue—in front of Kurt. When her son grew up and envisioned his future romantic partners, she wanted him to think of strong women like Maria Wylder. Not a woman who couldn't make ends meet without help from a man.

"Did he make his last child-support payment?" Brant whispered.

She shook her head. Heath was supposed to be paying her every week. So far, he hadn't done so beyond the first week, when he'd still believed that if he was Mr. Kind and Generous she'd come home again. He was now behind by two payments, three if money didn't arrive on Monday.

They'd married because it had been the right thing to do, both of them wanting to give Kurt the family they hadn't had. It hadn't worked out, so why the games?

Maybe because he needed her to figure out his rodeo stock contractor business accounts? Or because he knew how difficult it was to be a father to a boy he rarely saw? So far he'd rarely taken Kurt on his custody days, and then had brought him home early, both of them frustrated and angry.

What Heath didn't realize was that his games just made her even more determined to make it on her own. Before long she'd be on her feet again, and able to pay Brant rent as well as take a job outside his clinic—one where she was truly needed, and the work wasn't made up just so she'd have *something*.

Then she'd be ready. Ready for Brant and all he offered. And she'd do it as a partner, an equal.

And today, by not responding to Heath's games, she was beginning that change.

BRANT FELT A SHIFT IN APRIL. Every once in a while she would decide something, and her entire being would seem to somehow alter. Two years ago, he'd known she was planning to leave Heath a week before she'd told him. She'd lost her nerve, though, and had backed down when her husband had promised her he'd change.

The second time, more recently, Brant had seen that steel rod of determination settle in April's spine again, and he'd known she was ready to move on. All she'd needed was a safety net to land in, which he'd provided.

Today's shift was one he hadn't predicted, though, and he wasn't sure what it meant. She didn't want to spill her guts about Heath like usual, but it didn't feel as though she was blocking Brant out. Instead, it felt more like she was moving past her old hurts, healing, changing, and determined not to allow her ex to get to her.

Maybe she was closer to being ready for someone new than Brant had thought. He could see how her lack of independence was wearing on her, and like always, she was impatient to start her new life the way she envisioned it. He wasn't sure what he could do to help her, though.

They were sitting on the back step, watching Kurt play, their knees touching. They each had a cup of coffee, a swirl of steam rising into the cool air above their mugs.

"You know," he said, reaching inside his coat, "I got something for you, too." He pulled out a small wrapped box from the jewelry store in Riverbend and handed it to April.

"Oh," she breathed. She held it for a moment, looking at him. With pink cheeks she unwrapped the paper, then opened it. Inside, nestled in the padding, was an oval locket. Using her thumbnail, she opened it, and her eyes filled with tears as she spied the photo of her holding a newborn Kurt. April blinked, fighting a giant smile for about a split second before it broke free, her dimples flashing, her face lighting up.

She turned to Brant, set down her coffee and wrapped her arms around him. Holding him tightly, she whispered, "Thank you." Her voice was choked, and Brant hugged her back, savoring the way her curves fit and folded into him. She smelled like Christmas cookies and fresh air, new beginnings and hope.

"You're welcome." When the embrace ended, she tipped her chin up, and for a moment he thought they might kiss.

They held the pose for a long moment before she blushed and lowered her lashes.

Nope, not quite ready yet. He dropped his own eyes, beating back the surprisingly deep disappointment.

"Good things happen," he said, reminding her of their saying. Even in the bad times, good things did happen. Her marriage with Heath might not have worked out, but she had Kurt.

She looked up from the locket. "Silver linings?"

He smiled, and she returned it. He longed to kiss her, to stroke her cheek, but know it had to be on her terms, when she was ready.

But he really wished she was. As ready as he was.

APRIL SAT on the love seat near the Christmas tree in the Sweet Meadows Ranch living room, surrounded by Wylders. Christmas dinner would be served soon, and much to Kurt's delight, there had been gifts waiting for him here.

The Wylders were spoiling him, and he loved every minute. While Heath's and April's own families might not be active in Kurt's life, the Wylders made up for it every day. She'd missed them in the years she'd been with Heath, when she'd spent less time with them.

That afternoon, long after Brant had gone home, and after a rousing game of cops and robbers, April had convinced Kurt to come into the house to get ready for supper. He'd had lunch in his playhouse, and she had a feeling he was going to spend more hours in there during the coming weeks than he would inside their home.

The gift was perfect.

Just like Brant.

The man had been helping his mom in the kitchen, and now he paused in the middle of the living room as though deciding where to sit. The space was filled with family, love and happiness. Carly and Ryan were off to one side, gently arguing about something, Laura and Levi were snuggled up on the couch, and Karen and Myles were dancing to one of their grandfather Carmichael's records. Rumor was that Maria had even had a bit of a romance last week during her short vacation at a beach town in South Carolina.

She'd been quiet about it, and April felt for the woman, understanding how a whirlwind romance that seemed so full of adventure could leave such a painful aftermath. Before you knew it, you were tossed out with the dregs, the romance over. April had done that way too many times, and she wasn't doing it again.

New April coming through. She was going to take her time with Brant. No roller coaster rides. Their relationship would be a quiet buildup. No mistakes. No hoopla.

She had her son to think about if she and Brant got involved. Especially since Kurt was already calling him Daddy Brant.

She toyed with the locket Brant had given her, thinking about her plan to gain more independence. Every moment with him strengthened the confirmation that he was the man she had been waiting for, and she was impatient to get her life together and be with him.

She watched Brant, taking in the details of his build. He was broad shouldered and fit, his eyes soft and kind, that crazy Wylder blue. At the moment his brown hair was longer than his brothers' and it suited him. She knew he'd just been too busy to zip into the barber's, but it lent him a devil-may-care look, out of character and yet somehow perfect. Despite all her mistakes, this man still thought she was amazing, and wanted nothing but the best for her.

He was such a keeper, and it killed her knowing she'd missed seeing that in him for so many years. He'd been here. Right *here*.

April patted the cushion beside her when Brant looked her way. His expression brightened with surprise, then he came and joined her on the love seat, his moves smooth and at ease. Nearby, Kurt played on the floor with his farm set from Carmichael. April allowed her thigh to touch Brant's, enjoying the warmth and security of his presence.

He cleared his throat. "Hey."

"Hey, stranger." A burst of shyness overcame her. They'd almost kissed that afternoon in her yard, and she wished he would kiss her now, make them one of the loving couples in this room. But she knew it wasn't their time yet, no matter how much she believed she saw the desire in his steady gaze. They needed to move slowly, be sure.

Brant shifted on the love seat and she looked up as he gently grasped her chin, pulling her face toward him.

She knew what was coming, and despite her wishes to wait, felt a swell of anticipation and happiness. He wanted this. She wanted this. Could anything be more perfect?

Her lips parted as he angled in. Closer. Closer.

The kiss was soft, sending a wave of warmth through her. It was short, but filled her with so much hope for the future she wanted to throw her arms around him and kiss him deeper, longer. She wanted to know everything about him. Wanted to know how well they'd fit together in every aspect of a relationship, and if they'd go the distance.

Brant blinked and straightened. He looked surprised again, but also wary as he glanced around the room. April felt the gravity of what they'd done as awareness crept in. They'd kissed. In front of the family. In front of Kurt. She sucked in a small breath, hating that she always seemed to race into things and, as a result, ruin them. She glanced around the room in turn, her fear overtaking the dreamy aftereffect of the kiss.

What was everyone going to think about them kissing so soon after her divorce? How was Kurt going to react? What if getting involved was just part of Brant's rescue act? The one where he thought he was in love with her, like he had with Shelley St. Martin after college, when all she'd wanted was his help.

April scanned the room, waiting for a telltale smirk or stare to say the family thought they were making a mistake. Nothing. Nobody was looking at them. Nobody had seen the kiss.

She relaxed, keeping her lashes lowered while she sorted out her next move. She laced her fingers with Brant's, then slid their interlocked hands between them so nobody could see. She wanted him to know that the kiss hadn't been a mistake. That it had been welcomed, even though she wasn't ready to pursue more. She didn't want to mess this up, create rumors or hurt anyone.

He gave her hand a squeeze, but when she glanced up again, he was looking away.

Maria and Laura were talking about supper, but April couldn't focus. Then the front door opened and her friend Jackie Moorhouse came blowing in, out of breath and full of excitement as always. Henry Wylder, Carmichael's younger brother, came in as well, frowning and complaining about Jackie's driving. Around them the ranch's menagerie of dogs drifted in and out, preventing Henry from closing the door.

April struggled to focus on Jackie's banter, the others' laughter and why Brant was offering to help fix Jackie's car. April needed to drag him into a different room and figure this out. Right now. Her brain was screaming at her that she was repeating past mistakes, that she was rushing into things.

Jackie's eyes suddenly cut to the two of them. April held her breath, her hand still clutched in Brant's, out of sight.

"I saved you seats together at the football games," her friend announced. "Am I four-for-four?"

April's heart dropped at this blatant reference to Jackie's touted matchmaking skills. The feeling of losing control, of sliding into something she couldn't steer away from overtook her.

Before she or Brant could speak, Maria gasped loudly, and suddenly the focus was on the front doorway again, where April's ex-boyfriend stood, grinning as though he had only stepped out to do chores, not left town five years ago.

He'd left because April had asked for some space. And then he hadn't returned, despite multiple requests from his family. Now he was here. Moments after she'd kissed his sweet brother Brant.

As April's blood ran cold, then hot, then cold again, Cole said to Jackie, "Who did you save those seats for?"

His gaze moved through the room, landing on April's. She pulled her hand from Brant's, certain her past mistakes had finally caught up with her.

2

Five years away. Why was Cole here now? Brant had been tracking his brother across North America for years, intermittently asking him to come home. And literally moments after Brant finally kissed April MacFarlane, Cole's ex-girlfriend, his brother had decided to listen. Brant hadn't even processed the kiss, and where April might be mentally with this shift in their relationship, and then Jackie had come blasting in, followed by his missing brother.

Had Cole heard April was divorced, and come back for a second chance?

If so, he was definitely a jerk.

Brant caught himself narrowing his eyes at Cole amid the buoyant chatter and laughter. Everyone had gathered in the living room after their mother's amazing Christmas dinner, but neither Cole nor Brant had taken a seat.

Cole was telling tales of his adventures, which sounded intriguing. He'd always been a bit of a rascal, meaning chaos and upheaval would no doubt be the theme for the upcoming year, with him here. If the past was any indication, he'd find a way to suck April back into his personal undertow. The man was a riptide specially suited to her, just like her ex-husband, Heath. They drew her in with promises of adventure, only to shred her entire world. She'd changed, but Brant knew how strong the attraction could be despite her desire for stability.

With arms crossed, he shifted so that he was standing slightly in front of April, watching Cole work over the family.

His brother had left everyone five years ago. Left April, his ex-girlfriend, a woman who was family, pregnant, lost and hurt. He could have helped her navigate things with Heath. Instead he had left the ranch. Their brothers. Their mom. Their dad. Their aging grandfather. He'd even left his horse.

He'd abandoned them all because he couldn't face the tough stuff, and now that the smoke was clearing, thanks to Brant, he'd returned as if nothing had happened.

He was acting as though he still belonged here.

And the worst part was that, despite it all, he did.

But he no longer belonged with April.

Brant did. And he was going to make sure his brother knew it.

"WE SHOULD TALK," April said, snagging Brant's shirtsleeve as he passed her in the living room after supper, his attention focused on Cole.

He paused, watching her. "Okay."

She glanced around the room. With the meal and most of the cleanup completed, almost everyone had filtered into the living room. She needed somewhere private where they discuss things without raising suspicions about the two of them.

"Well, am I going to get a hug or what?" Cole asked just then, his cowboy boots echoing across the tile floor as he crossed the room. April stiffened when he pulled her into a brief embrace that was familiar yet uncomfortable. Whatever had been between them was gone. Long gone. Relief swept through her as she realized that the attraction of Cole's touch, once powerful, had died.

She straightened her spine,, shortening the hug. Since the day she'd moved to the Sweet Meadows Ranch as a five-year-old with her ranch-hand dad, she'd had a crush on Cole. She'd grown up yearning to be important enough that the second Wylder boy, older than her by two years, would want to have her at his side, even though he could have any gal on the rodeo circuit riding shotgun in his pickup.

But that crush had died long ago, as had her desire to be noticed by him. Hugging him now, she'd felt none of that old desperate attraction that had once characterized her feelings for Cole. She was ready for something settled, her powerful need for excitement gone. Something had shifted inside her, and she realized that, emotionally, she might be way more ready for something with Brant than she'd previously thought.

"So you'll be around for a bit?" Brant asked his brother.

"We'll see." Cole held April at arm's length, his eyes likely tracking every change that time and motherhood had brought. Especially the fifty pounds that made even her new clothes fit snugly.

April politely eased herself from his grip. Like Brant's, Cole's dark hair didn't show a hint of plans to recede, despite his thirty-three years. He still had those crazy electric-blue eyes, although to April they didn't have the depth Brant's did. The last hints of youth had faded in the years Cole was away, leaving what seemed to be a solid, self-assured adult. He was handsome like his brothers, but lacked that calm warmth that drew her to Brant. There was something about the way Brant quietly watched her, a soft smile teasing his lips, that would make her heart flutter and feel the urge to smother him with kisses.

She inhaled, reminding herself that she needed to go slowly with Brant. Even though coming face to face with her past, aka

Cole, made her want to run to Brant that much faster, to capture that special thing they seemed to have growing between them.

"I didn't realize you were coming home," April said mildly. Brant was at her side, shifting closer, and she got the impression he was struggling with the urge to put a possessive arm around her.

Cole's semi-cocky expression slipped, and she realized his comfortable bravado had been an act. Cole Wylder, the most confident man she'd ever known, was feeling uncertain in his own family home. Somewhere along the lines, this had become her turf, and he wasn't sure he was welcome.

But why?

When she'd discovered she was pregnant with Heath's baby after their rebound relationship, a few months after her final breakup with Cole, she'd been afraid she'd get wound up in Cole and his ideas on what she should do. She'd asked him for some space—just a few months—so she could sort out how she felt about Heath. He'd granted her five years.

It made little sense, as did the quiet sorrow in his eyes, telling her there was more to his absence than her simple request for some breathing room.

"This is your home. You're always welcome here," she said.

He snorted, a soft sound that resembled hurt. Emotion flickered across his face before he tamped it back. April glanced at Brant, glimpsing Levi in the background. Both had looked away from Cole when he'd snorted.

Something was definitely going on here.

"This is where you belong," she affirmed.

"Do I?" He crossed his arms protectively.

"I didn't ask you to leave." She'd asked for space. Enough that she could give Heath a chance, without being drawn back into the familiar turbulence of dating Cole. "I don't know why you—" The room had grown silent and April abruptly bit her tongue.

Just like old times, within the space of a few words they were heading straight from a civil conversation to locking horns. It was so obvious to her now that they were a poor fit. It was like trying to fit a metric nut on an imperial bolt.

"Let's all just take a breath," Brant said, exhaling slowly as though to demonstrate. "You've both moved on, and you're both different people now. And Cole, I'm sure Levi's glad to have you back on the ranch again."

Cole sent him another assessing look, this one longer. Brant stood beside April, shoulders back, ready to defend her.

Her heart swelled even as her brain reminded her that women who had their lives together did not need rescue by wonderful men like Brant.

"I'm going to help your mom finish up in the kitchen," she muttered, letting the brothers face off on their own.

"So? What's up with you and Brant? And you and Cole?" Jackie whispered, falling into step beside her, an empty dip bowl in hand.

"Nothing and nothing."

Her friend twisted her lips in disbelief, and April sighed. She was sure to be the topic of some pretty juicy gossip in the coming days, with Cole's sudden return. Especially so shortly after her divorce.

"I'm different now," April said forcefully. "*Everything* is different." She was no longer that needy gal who got sucked in by Cole's adventures, then turned around only to find herself spit out on her hands and knees.

And she was no longer interested in doing the same thing to him, either.

"Brant was ready to haul you away like a caveman. So hot!" Jackie fanned herself.

"I can take care of myself."

"I know," Jackie said simply. Her voice dropped as she asked hesitantly, "Did he ask you for a second chance?"

"Cole? No." April stopped in the kitchen doorway, giving her friend a look of disgust.

Jackie's hands flew up and she shrank back with an uneasy giggle."Just asking." She lowered her voice again. "So you and Brant then? He's the kind of guy who could have any woman in town running down the aisle, with nothing more than a nod and a smile."

April let that vision soak in before shaking it off. "It's just…" She leaned her head against the door frame, thinking about Brant and that wonderful kiss, and how she felt so certain he was the one. "It's complicated. I'm not in the right place to start something serious, but on the other hand, a big part of me is *so* ready."

Jackie grinned. "Girlfriend, buckle up, because when you two become a 'you two' that news will spread like wildfire."

"And if we don't?"

"That's going to spread like wildfire, too." She tipped her head toward Cole.

April sighed. Either way, it looked like she'd be spreading some fiery gossip. The question was, what kind should she create? Did she want to make it look like Brant had broken up her marriage? Or that Cole was back for a second chance?

As she peeked around the corner into the living room, she spied Brant tucking a blanket over her sleepy-looking son. Kurt had been playing with toys on his stomach, and now, unmoving, had his head resting on his arm.

Yes, if April MacFarlane was going to star in some wildfire gossip, she knew exactly what kind of rumors she wanted to start. And it wasn't either of the two previous options. It was something much more heart-lifting and sweet, something about two people finally falling in love with the person they were meant to be with.

"YOU'RE STILL April's big defender, huh?" Cole asked, after April left the room with Jackie.

Brant sized up his brother. He was tanned despite it being December, hinting that he hadn't come from the north—Blueberry Springs, Colorado, the last place Brant had tracked him to. Over the past several years, his brother had put on miles as if he was being chased.

"Levi said you bought her a house," Cole stated.

Brant hooked his thumbs in his belt loops and turned to face him more fully. Cole didn't understand that sometimes it wasn't about usurping independence when you took action, but listening and then taking care of the tough stuff. Not taking over or walking away. "I'm *helping* her. She's *family.*"

It was worth going into debt to provide her and Kurt with safe shelter. And it was worth stretching his clinic's budget to hire her as extra help. There was no way he'd ever regret doing that.

"You were always there for her," Cole said thoughtfully, his tone tinged with something that might be regret. "Letting her cry on your shoulder."

Brant had a flash of insight. "You're jealous."

His brother crossed his arms even more tightly across his chest, his shoulders hunched. "Nope."

Brant continued to stare at him as memories fell into place, creating a picture. All those times April had come crying to him after Cole had done this, that or the other thing to cause another breakup had actually eaten Cole up inside.

"I just wanted to say thanks for being there for her," Cole said, his voice gruff. "As a friend."

"Always," he replied, bristling at the pointed reminder of how many years he'd found himself in the friend zone.

Cole's gaze had fallen on Jackie Moorhouse as she reentered the room. Her eyes widened, her face flushed and she spun on her heel, muttering about helping in the kitchen. She disappeared around the corner on stiff legs.

"She's been real quiet," Cole stated.

Brant kept his mouth shut. Jackie was still a matchmaking, meddlesome and endearing brat who had never in her life been described as quiet. She'd had her eye on the Wylder brothers since elementary school, and twenty years later, Brant bet that Cole was her pick of the litter.

"Didn't she used to talk a lot?" Cole asked, still watching the kitchen doorway.

"She still does." She was bubbly, effusive and a ton of fun. "She's single, you know."

"She never wrangled someone into meeting her in Old Man Lovely's chapel on New Year's Eve?"

Brant shook his head.

"Does he still do that?" Cole asked.

"Every year."

The Texas legal system still had the odd old statute sticking to the books, such as the unlawfulness of milking someone else's cow, and how if two willing parties publicly announced that they were married, and did so three times, then it was considered official. In their little spot in Texas, Grant Lovely had retained the authority to marry couples without them going through the usual licensing rigamarole. It was a legal loophole left over from the days of shotgun weddings. Rumor had it that Old Man Lovely was the last living person with such authority in the state. And each New Year's Eve he would exercise that ability by turning on the lights in his six-person chapel located on his property near the swimming hole, and marrying one couple. The next morning the Sweetheart Creek newspaper, now online, would announce the year's newlyweds, and their photo would be framed and hung on a wall in the town office. There'd be a reception in the community barn and gifts would flood in.

There had been some embarrassing, poor decisions made

over the years. And naturally, the town found that to be most entertaining.

"And do you still pimp yourself out as a fake boyfriend to help women with persistent exes?" Cole asked with an amused chuckle, his shoulders relaxing.

Brant scowled. There had never been any pimping or anything untoward. It had always been just a nice thing to do.

Cole slapped him on the back. "Some things never change, huh? You're a good man." He glanced toward the kitchen doorway where Jackie had disappeared. "Except she's cuter. Why is she here for Christmas?"

"Her dad's in a nursing home now, so she had an early supper over there, but typically joins us for the holidays. You heard Connie passed?" he asked, referring to Jackie's mother. Cole nodded. "Jackie's going to her brother's in Dallas tomorrow. They're at his in-laws tonight."

"Remember when she used to chase us around at recess?" Cole smiled at the memory.

"I'm pretty sure she'd still chase you around, if you were game."

Cole's lips pursed slightly as though he might be considering the idea. He shifted his focus back to Brant. "She's barely said a word to me." He glanced back again when Jackie reentered the room.

Come to think of it, she had been quiet since Cole's arrival, Brant realized. Earlier, she'd blasted into the Christmas dinner gathering like a storm, full of laughter and teasing. She'd given their great-uncle a ride over, and had hit the ditch in order to miss Bill, the neighborhood armadillo. Uncle Henry had been gruff and upset, but Jackie had shaken it all off with a smile and said she'd duct tape her car's bumper back into place later.

"You've taken us all by surprise," Brant said mildly, as Jackie collected drinking glasses in need of washing.

"You told me to come back," Cole mumbled, his eyes still tracking her. "How could this be a surprise?"

"That was what? Eight months ago? Nine?" Had it really been that long since he'd flown all the way to Blueberry Springs in an attempt to convince Cole to return for their father's June wedding?

Cole lifted his chin toward the Christmas tree, where Myles, Levi and their girlfriends were chatting with Carmichael and Uncle Henry. And the local mechanic, Clint Walker.

"What's the story with Mom and Mr. Walker?"

"Clint? He and Mom have been spending some time together lately."

Their mother had gone to Indigo Bay, South Carolina, a week ago, and so had Clint. Rumor was they'd gone on some dates, but Maria had come back upset and silent. Tonight, however, she was smiling widely. Was that because of Clint or Cole?

"I used to believe nothing ever changed around here," Cole mused. "But now that I've been away, I see that everything has. Except you and your rescue complex." He grinned at Brant, baiting him, ruffling his feathers. Brant had missed that. Almost.

He played his old card, the insulted younger brother. "Excuse me?"

"You know, saving the dog Bonkers when he broke his leg and dad wanted to put him down, taking in strays, rescuing Shelley St. Martin and now April." He shrugged. "It's not a bad thing."

"I'm not rescuing April. She's perfectly capable of taking care of herself." Brant cringed internally. He *was* rescuing her, but it was because he cared and she'd found herself stuck.

And Shelley? Well, Brant had thought they'd found true love, but it turned out she'd just needed him to set her life back on its wheels so she could peel off into the sunset. April wasn't going to peel off anywhere. She liked him for reasons beyond his ability to help her out of a jam.

Anyway, the growing rapport between himself and April differed from how things had been with Shelley. April's kiss hadn't been one of gratitude, but charged with attraction. Sweet, yes, but with an unexpected jolt of heat that made him want to kiss her again. And then some more, just to see what the follow-up kisses would be like.

Ryan and Carly entered from the kitchen, carrying bottles of his homemade brew. "Beer?" he offered, extending a selection clustered in his fingers.

"Thanks," Brant said, carefully choosing a pale ale and avoiding the Lambic brew that his brother fermented using natural yeasts pulled from the ranch's country air. It tasted as bad as the idea sounded. There might be a way to pull off the idea, but Ryan had yet to discover it.

Cole barely looked at the various choices, taking the closest bottle as April entered the room. Ryan and Brant shared a smirk as Cole uncapped a Lambic beer. Ryan continued the rounds, offering beverages to all. Brant noticed he'd brought out only one Lambic, which meant his prankster youngest brother was still up to his usual tricks.

Cole tracked April with his gaze as she cruised through the living room looking for dishes in need of washing. Brant's own eyes lit on her and stayed. There was something about her that drew him in. Her strength and get-it-done attitude, her generous smiles and quick wit. She was an amazing mom, and an intuitive receptionist in his veterinarian clinic. He'd known her since she was five, and it still felt as though he was learning new things about her daily. He didn't think that would ever stop.

"She's, uh…curvier now," Cole mused, as April disappeared into the kitchen.

"She's sexy," Brant growled, his fist tightening around his beer bottle. He liked her curves. Even more so because they were due to having the son she so clearly loved.

"Wow." Cole appraised him, eyebrows raised, his free hand lifted in defense. "Thought you would have outgrown that thing you had for her." Watching for Brant's reaction, he raised the bottle of Ryan's homemade beer to his lips. His face pinched with displeasure as he got a taste of it, and over by the tree, Ryan snickered.

Brant took a sip of his own carefully chosen pale ale and thanked karma for this small moment of triumph over his older brother. "She's an amazing woman," he said, feeling a tad smug.

"I know," Cole replied.

"She's getting her life together. It's not a good time for you to come in and do your thing."

"My thing?" Cole turned, squaring his shoulders to Brant's as though ready to fight. "What makes you think I've come here to meddle in her life?"

"Haven't you?"

"No, actually. I haven't." Cole's posture shifted, so he was taking up more space. "And what's your deal? You speak for her now? Make her decisions? She's not going to like that, you know."

"I don't speak for her, and you know what I mean. You rip her up. You think you're showing her a good time, but you don't see her afterward. Anytime you go near her, there are pieces that need putting back together."

Cole inhaled, his spine straightening. Brant thought for a second his brother might take a swing at him. Instead, Cole's shoulders dropped, and he gave a slow nod of acceptance.

"She was never a good match for you," Brant said, knowing he was pushing the limits, but needing his brother to grasp the fact that any chance he might think he had with April had disappeared when he'd left town.

"We had a lot of fun though." Cole smiled, lifting the bottle to his lips before he thought twice and lowered it again.

"And that fun had consequences."

"Kurt's not mine. You know that." There was a flash in Cole's eyes. One that warned of an upcoming fight. Brant understood that Kurt wasn't Cole's, despite the odd rumor still swirling around town that he might be. To Brant it didn't matter; he wasn't fighting for April's honor or anything that antiquated. She could do that herself. He was fighting for *her*. Period.

"Emotional consequences," he said.

"You really think I'm here to stir things up?" Cole seemed hurt.

Brant didn't answer.

"You know," his brother said after a moment, "she just got divorced and is living in your house."

"She's not Shelley."

"I didn't say she was." His voice was low. "But you realize you might be making your own pieces?"

"You think *I'm* a threat to her emotional well-being?" Brant struggled against the anger that rose within him like lava. He'd never been one to choose fists, but he found himself considering the ways he might take Cole, a fighter, down.

His brother shrugged, his steady gaze meeting Brant's. "You break up her marriage to Heath?"

"Heath was a rebound relationship that went wrong," Brant stated. There was a tightening of the jaw, nothing more. "You could have made things better if you hadn't run. If you'd stayed. If you'd loved her enough to face your own fears."

Cole's nostrils flared. But he had obviously gotten better at holding some things in, letting others go. Five years before he'd nearly decked Brant for butting in and advising him to stay with April and help her through the pregnancy. Cole had shouted and fumed at Brant. The next day he'd been gone before dawn.

"You still think it would've been better for me to stay?" He was holding back anger, but the question in his eyes was real. He wanted to know.

Brant stared at him, imagining a different future. One where Cole had stuck around and kept April from marrying Heath, preventing that mistake.

"No. Because if you'd stayed, I don't think she would have

become who she is today." The woman he was falling for more and more with each passing day.

APRIL HURRIED to get Kurt ready to go, thanking Maria for Christmas dinner as she did so. Less than ten minutes ago, Brant had walked Carmichael over to his house, the original homestead located just on the other side of the holly hedge, not more than a minute away. When he'd returned, he'd glanced around the room, seen her talking with Cole, who'd been trying to apologize for their past mistakes, then waved his cell phone in the air, saying he had to leave due to an animal emergency. She wasn't sure if the family had seen through the fib, but she had. And not just because he wasn't the veterinarian on call for his clinic tonight.

Something was going on with Brant, and she intended to find out what. She stepped into the dark, crisp December night, Myles, the middle Wylder brother, carrying a sleepy Kurt for her. Cattle were bellowing in a nearby pasture, a horse whinnying in one of the stables. Everything about outside sounded and felt like home.

As the door closed behind them, April caught sight of Brant standing beside his truck, which had the mobile veterinarian unit in back. He gave a small shrug, and she grinned.

"Didn't think that one through, did you?" she teased. "Where ya gonna go, Wylder? It's Christmas."

A pang of guilt jabbed her. It was likely her fault he didn't want to be in the house with his family right now. But it was also definitely her fault he was smiling as they met up in front of her SUV.

She opened the back door for Myles, who was still carrying Kurt, but he handed her son off to Brant.

"Faked another animal emergency?" Myles said kindly to his brother.

Brant's lips twisted in a wry smile, and Myles chuckled under his breath. "Don't blame you. That was no doubt awkward for the three of you." He began walking back to the house, calling over his shoulder, "See y'all later."

April's cheeks warmed as Brant's eyes met hers. Kurt snuggled in his arms as if he belonged there, and all she could think of was her son calling him Daddy Brant earlier in the day. All the Wylders were great with Kurt, but Brant was something else. His kindness extended from the animal world to the smallest human creatures, and they responded to him in a way that made her love him all the more.

Brant folded Kurt into his seat and buckled him up. By the time he was done, Myles was back in the house, leaving April and Brant alone.

They faced each other in the dim glow from the yard light, neither speaking.

"I was thinking," April said.

He started to say at the same time, "I don't want this to be..."

"You go first," she told him, when he paused.

"No, ladies first."

"Don't give me that." April propped her hands on her hips.

They stood in silence for another long moment.

"It's something, having Cole come back, huh?" Brant said at last, and she sighed, wishing he'd expressed whatever was on his mind.

"I'm not ready."

"For him to be home?" Brant shifted, almost as if he planned to go grab his brother by the collar and toss him out on his ear.

"For a relationship," she blurted, swallowing over the lump that had appeared in her throat when she tried to add, "For us."

There was a beat of silence, but it wasn't that comfortable pause they'd known as teens, when they could sit by the creek and watch the water tumble over the rocks for hours, picking up threads of conversation here and there. They'd been happy to speak, happy to remain silent. Back then it was as though time slowed down to the pace of a butterfly fluttering past. Today it felt like it was racing by.

"Yeah, sorry," Brant said. "I got confused."

"Confused?"

"I got caught up in the whole rescue thing. You know how I do that. Thinking things are real, but it's just gratitude." He hadn't stepped away, but stood there calmly, his gaze steady on her lips, as though wishing she'd correct him.

"Yeah, me too," she replied, feeling breathless, knowing this was the conversation she'd wanted to have. To fix things. To set parameters so this didn't crash and burn on them. She was leaning close, and his hand, strong from hard work, rested on her hip. "I got confused, too. I'm trying to change."

"Why?"

"I'm trying to be independent so you don't have to rescue me anymore. I want to meet you halfway, so that whatever this is works. For real." A frantic feeling clawed its way up inside her again at the thought of getting things wrong, of losing control of what felt important between them.

He shifted closer. "Halfway?"

The frantic sensation slowly eased. Brant was the one man who would never deny her whatever it was she needed in order to be whole. Her voice was small when she asked, "Will you wait for me to be ready?"

His forehead lowered to hers as they sighed in unison, their breath creating misty clouds that melted away like her resolve often did. Both his hands were on her waist now, her own resting against his chest.

"That way when we get together we'll know you're not rescuing me." Her lips were near his, their bodies shifting, bringing them close enough to kiss.

He gave a small hum of agreement.

"We won't start nasty rumors, either," she added.

"I can handle them." His focus was taut, zeroed in on her mouth, and her heart lifted and opened.

"I know, but I'm trying to save you from the full April MacFarlane experience."She was up on her tiptoes now, gripping his jacket in her hands.

"Why would you do that? I like her," he murmured.

"She's a mess."

"Maybe I like messes."

She slid her arms across his shoulders, embracing him, savoring the sensation of having her body pressed against his. "You enjoy cleaning them up."

"Especially when it involves something like this."

His lips lowered to hers in a long, sweet kiss that left April breathless and wondering why on earth she had ever thought waiting was a good idea.

The next kiss was hungry, with a passion and heat building and growing until they finally broke apart, panting.

"Oh," she whispered. "Wow." She slowly stepped away, her fingers pressed to her lips. She had never been kissed like that, with such sureness and fire.

Brant had her back in his arms in a heartbeat, and they angled their mouths, kissing deeper.

This? This was going to be amazing.

"That's what we're waiting for," Brant said at last, breaking the embrace and putting distance between them again.

April had never been so impatient in all her life.

3

*S*itting behind the large reception desk at Call of the Wyld(er), Brant's veterinarian clinic, April was filing the morning's animal medical records when the bell above the door jingled. Her friend Jackie entered, wearing such a gigantic grin that April wondered if Cole had asked her out. The two would make a great couple, their lively personalities well suited for each other.

"So?" Jackie asked meaningfully, leaning against the tall counter in front of April's desk.

"Hi y'all!" Her ponytail swinging, cup of coffee from the diner in hand, Jenny Oliver entered. "I saw Jackie come in." The owner of the Blue Tumbleweed clothing shop smiled at them, obviously ready to swap holiday gossip.

"What's the latest chatter out there?" April asked cautiously. She had a feeling the best scuttlebutt would be about her, and her friends were here to get the truth straight from the horse's mouth.

"Maria and Clint are an item," Jenny offered.

April and Jackie nodded.

"And Cole came home for you." Jenny looked at April.

"I heard she kissed Brant," Jackie exclaimed. She turned to face April, rapping her pink nails on the countertop. "Cole asked you back?"

"No," April declared, with enough disgust that her friends frowned. "Sorry, but no. Neither of us are going down that path again."

"Because Brant kissed you?" Jackie asked, a hopeful tone lifting her voice.

April rolled her eyes, knowing her cheeks were glowing. The first kiss by the Christmas tree had been brief and sweet, and yet somehow unlike anything else. But then the ones later that night? The ones Brant said were to show her what she was waiting for?

Those were the subject of fantasies.

Brant's kisses weren't a demand. They were indescribable. They didn't take; they didn't strip a woman dry. They were magical, healing and addictive.

She needed to think about something else, because the way those kisses were still burning through her system like a drug was sure to be obvious to the women on the other side of the counter.

But in the three days since Christmas, she and Brant hadn't kissed. Not once.

They'd agreed that wouldn't happen, because she'd asked him to wait.

What had she been thinking?

She cleared her throat, strengthened her resolve and said, "I'm not ready for a relationship." She lowered her voice, glancing at the door behind her that led to the surgery, where Brant was fixing a dog's torn dew claw. "So, just… You know…"

Donna Nestner, the mayor's wife, entered the clinic, the doorway bell ringing. "Howdy, gals! How was your Christmas? I heard yours was merry, with a little kissing under the mistletoe with two different Wylders." She winked at April.

Jackie shot April an innocent look, as if to say it hadn't been her starting the rumors.

"Not true." April sighed as the other women shared doubtful glances.

"What can I get for you today?" she asked Donna.

"Just some of that doggie toothpaste. Munchkin has tartar buildup again," she replied, referring to her triplets' pet.

"It's on the shelf over here," April said, getting up to show her.

"I'll grab it." She placed a tube on the counter. "Did Travis tell you the Hill Country Community College is doing an animal husbandry study? He's hoping to get some ranchers on board as well as a vet from our area. Would Brant be interested?"

"I'll ask." April knew Brant had been approached already, but since the project was obviously up his alley, nobody seemed too eager to take his "too busy" excuse as his final answer.

"So when are you going to be ready for a relationship?" Jackie asked April. "Because someone around town seems *very* interested." She tilted her head toward the back of the clinic.

Donna and Jenny leaned in, all ears.

"He's only doing his rescue thing." April worked on ringing up Donna's toothpaste purchase, in hopes of hiding the way her face had heated with the partial lie. She knew Brant was interested in her. She just wasn't certain how much was genuine attraction and how much was due to her needing his help.

"Yeah, sure he is," Jackie said skeptically.

"We've seen the way he looks at you," Jenny added with a wistful sigh.

"My marriage just ended," April said, reaching for an excuse, and hoping her friends would play devil's advocate and convince her that Brant's attraction was one hundred percent real. "It would be a rebound relationship. And you know how that worked out for me last time." She tapped the debit machine to get Donna's attention, so she'd start paying for the toothpaste.

"So you and Brant aren't an item?" the mayor's wife asked, her brow furrowed, the device slack in her grip. "Everyone's talking about you and Cole, since, you know… The divorce and all, and Kurt needing a daddy."

"Kurt isn't Cole's," April said, her heart beating faster at the thought of her son overhearing someone speculating about his parentage.

"Oh, I know," Donna said quickly. "People are just talking, that's all." She gave April a sympathetic look. "You know how the gossips can be."

"Maybe you need to get obvious with Brant," Jackie suggested with a sly smile.

"That would kill the rumors about Cole trying to win you back, or returning to be a daddy." Jenny nodded thoughtfully.

"And getting close with Brant would help Heath take a hint, too," Jackie said.

"Is he still bothering you?" Donna asked worriedly.

"It's fine. Really." Heath was playing games, but he wasn't an evil ex. April tore Donna's receipt from the debit machine, unable to erase the idea of how following her heart with Brant might help quell some of the rumors that might confuse Kurt. It would also likely help to settle her feelings of uncertainty around Brant's attraction, as she'd learned from experience that there was nothing like a relationship to show two people whether or not their attraction had any staying power.

"You and Brant would make a wonderful couple," Jenny said with a small smile. Donna and Jackie nodded.

April glanced over her shoulder to make sure Brant wasn't about to enter the reception area. "If I get involved with a certain someone so soon, I'm afraid everyone will think he broke up my marriage."

"Heath was never the man for you," Jackie said dismissively.

Donna placed her debit card back in her purse. "That marriage was all about doing the right thing. I've seen the way you and Brant look at each other, and that is *something*. Something good."

"But she says she's on the rebound," Jackie said, narrowing her eyes at April, obviously trying to think of a loophole. April found herself leaning forward, ready to hear it.

"So, technically, since you and Heath had a marriage borne out of duty, you wouldn't be on the rebound with Brant, right?" Jenny suggested.

Jackie's eyes widened with glee and she high-fived the shop owner. April couldn't help but smile. Her friends wanted something good for her, and were making some very compelling arguments. Ones she'd already had with herself on numerous occasions. Still, she knew it would be best to wait a while before diving into something.

"Y'all, I appreciate it, but... me and Brant are still a no." At the moment.

The trio gave her pleading looks that made her laugh. "Must I remind you he's my boss?" she asked lightly.

"Do you need me to get you fired?" Jackie whispered. She began looking around as though seeking something to destroy, then blame on April.

April choked on a bubble of laughter, with one thought bouncing through her head in a panic-inducing chant. Having a job was more important than a boyfriend at the moment.

"No, don't," she said to Jackie. "I'm just leaning on Brant a lot right now, and getting involved would complicate things. I want to be a strong partner, you know?"

Donna nodded. "I get it."

Jackie and Jenny looked confused.

"I have a son to think about. I can't afford to mess up with the man who's keeping us from living in a gutter somewhere."

"Oh, pish-posh," Jackie said with a frown. "You could come live with me."

"Or me," Jenny offered.

"Or join the Nestner zoo," Donna said with a fond smile.

Jackie was watching April, her lips, glossed a pretty shade of pink that matched her nails, pursed to one side. "So let's backtrack a sec. You think you're going to mess up?"

Donna shook her head, saying with authority, "Life's different when you're with the right man." She gave a small wave and headed for the door. "Wish I could chat longer, but I've got to pick up the girls. Happy New Year, if I don't see you at the Longhorn." She glanced back and whispered loudly, "Kiss him at midnight!"

The women laughed, and April rolled her eyes as she joined in.

"Happy New Year," the three echoed back as Donna exited.

Jackie brightened suddenly. "There's the hunky-hunk we're talking about!"

April closed her eyes, fearing Brant might have overheard something.

And why did her mind refuse to let go of the idea that it would all work out if he was the right man?

"All good things, I hope?" Brant asked. He was wearing a white lab coat that made him look like a walking contradiction. He was a cowboy, science geek and medical man. Competent, strong, smart, and a bit nerdy in all the ways that turned her crank.

She caught herself ogling him like a woman on a diet who could think only of cake, cake, cake. But in her case it was Brant, Brant, Brant.

"You can call Ripley's owners," he said, setting a folder down beside her. "Tell them he's doing well, and they can pick him up at four."

April nodded and moved Ripley's file near the phone so she'd remember to call once her friends left.

Brant placed his left hand on the armrest of April's chair, leaning forward to pull another folder from a box near her feet where he was keeping seasonal breeding results of local cattle. A hint of his aftershave filled her nostrils, the same scent that helped her identify which lab jacket to give him when he needed her to run one to him out in the birthing suite off the back of the building. She'd lift the jackets to her nose and inhale. When she reached the right one—Brant's—memories would warm her and she'd find herself smiling. Every time. If he ever got around to stitching his name across the pocket he'd deprive her of one of her favorite work tasks.

"Donna was asking about the study again," April said. She could feel her friends watching her interaction with Brant, and she studiously kept her focus on her desk.

Brant's right hand brushed her calf as he bent and reached, causing April's lungs to forget how to work properly. She could scoot her chair out of his way, but he was using it for support, his body solidly in her personal space and making it even more difficult to recall how to breathe. There was something terrifyingly alluring about his muscular forearms, wide shoulders and the capable gleam in his eyes when he smiled at her as he slowly straightened, file in hand. He was toying with her. Tempting her. Reminding her of… She didn't know what, but it felt illicit.

"I told her you're busy," she squeaked, realizing that at some point she'd become distracted and zeroed in on Brant and nothing else.

"Thanks." He waved the folder. "Levi's out back to talk cows." He nodded at Jackie and Jenny. "Ladies."

He returned to the back of the clinic, leaving sparks still zipping through April from his innocent, accidental touch. She let out a long, shuddery breath.

When she looked up, Jackie was watching her with a slightly evil smile.

"No. Don't even…" April began. "We can't. We work together."

Jenny was grinning broadly. "I may have a job coming open at my shop in the New Year. I'll put you at the top of my list."

BRANT WRANGLED a new washing machine for April onto the tailgate of the ranch's faded red pickup truck. The day after Christmas, the machine that had come with the house had finally met its maker.

The new washer was still in its box, and Brant was fairly confident he could slide it to the ground without disaster. They weren't as heavy as they'd been a few decades ago, technology stripping weight from the machine. He laid the box on its side and scooted it so the heavy bottom overhung the tailgate. From the ground, he tipped the box upright, his palms flat against its side as he eased it slowly to the ground.

The box suddenly slipped left, almost out of his reach. Hands smaller than his own caught the bottom edge.

"You could have asked for help, you know," April said as she worked with him to lower the box onto the street in front of her house. She smelled like sunshine and roses, and he debated ways to keep her closer for longer. She'd been extra shy since Christmas, and he wasn't sure if she regretted their kiss or was serious about needing more time. He had a feeling it was the latter.

"When did you get here?" He'd stuck his head into the reception area at the beginning of their lunch break and overheard MayBeth Albright asking about April and Cole. When Brant's fingers had begun to ache from clenching his hands, he'd decided it was best he head to April's rather than wait for her to continue to explain that she and Cole were history. He hadn't quite escaped before he heard MayBeth asking about himself and April, and if they were out in the open now that her divorce had been finalized. He'd nearly gotten a speeding ticket on his way over, his anger funneling through his foot.

He figured MayBeth's statement had likely negated any of the positive encouragement April's friends had made that morning while trying to convince her to date him. He'd quite liked the tidbits he'd overheard. Maybe he could ask them to come back for a second round.

"I got here just before you dropped this pretty new baby on the cold hard concrete," April said, rubbing her hands together in the weak December sun after setting the box down. "Let's get it in the house and hooked up."

"Merry Christmas," he teased.

"You already bought me something." Her fingers slipped to the locket hanging around her neck, accessible through her barely zipped up jacket. "But two thoughtful gifts? You spoil me so."

She was leaning close, and he considered kissing her. Instead, he caught himself, inhaling slowly, knowing he had a tendency to run in heart first and hit walls. He didn't want to do that with April. He wanted to get it right. And she'd said she wasn't ready. They'd kissed like they were inventing a new sin, but since then they'd remained hands-off.

It was her call, her move.

"I don't plan to stop spoiling you."

Her cheeks reddened and her shoulder touched his. Then her eyes shifted to their feet and she turned away, her shoulder still against his.

She peeked up at him, her nose crinkled. "You mean rescuing me?"

"No," he said fiercely, shaking his head. "This is different."

He could see the hesitation, the hint of doubt darkening the amber flecks in her eyes.

This was real. More real than it had been with Shelley or anyone else. And for him it had been like this for years. He couldn't fake what he felt.

Even if April hadn't needed his help, he would still be here, trying to win her heart.

She was gnawing on her lower lip and finally let out a long

sigh. "You don't have to help set it up. I can handle it." She dropped her palms on the box.

He placed his hands beside hers and leaned in, close enough to kiss. "You're going to wrangle this into the house and into place? What will you do with the old machine?"

"I thought it would make a beautiful planter in the front yard after I boot it off the front step." Her chin went up and she gave him a defiant smirk.

He chuckled and retrieved the dolly from the back of the truck. "You know, it'll take a lot more than that to get rid of me and my help. *And…*" He paused to make sure she didn't interrupt. "…accepting my help doesn't mean you can't take care of things on your own. But this is a two-person job."

April's gaze caught on something across the street. Brant turned. A neighbor was watering a potted shrub with her garden hose, water spilling over the rim and running down the walk as she gawked and leaned closer, trying to eavesdrop.

"We'd better get this inside before we start some rumors. Unless you'd like me to bend you over in a sensuous kiss that'll have Mrs. Jullium hustling into the house and calling in a complaint to the sheriff about public decency."

April's face turned red and she laughed. "Maybe not today."

"Okay, but know the offer's always open."

"Thanks."

Her tone was light, but he noted how her chest rose and fell as if she was battling an inner heat, like he was. Focusing on the job at hand rather than the sexy woman beside him, he rolled the washing machine to April's front door like a deliveryman. Wordlessly, she helped secure the heavy box on the cart as they nudged it up the steps, then held the door for him before he steered the machine to the small nook under the stairs on the main floor.

"They're going to talk no matter what we do," he said, as he began extracting the washer from its packing.

"I know," April replied. "I can handle this, though."

"I know."

"I mean, I'm sure you have other things to do with your lunch break."

"Trying to get rid of me?"

She pushed her bangs away from her eyes. They flopped back into place, endearingly crooked. "No, but maybe you need to live your life."

He narrowed his gaze, trying to sort out what she was getting at. Maybe she regretted those kisses, after all.

"I am living my life." He was exactly where he wanted to be right now.

"You could help more animals—which is totally your thing—instead of me." She lifted her brows. "That college study? They need a vet and a rancher from the area, and you check off both boxes."

"Maybe I have more pressing things to do with my time."

She laughed. "More important than taking care of cows?"

"Yes. And why is that funny?" He gripped the plastic strapping she was trying to slide off the box. She tugged at it, but he didn't let go.

"It's not. I just don't want you to spend all your time helping me, and then eventually resenting me."

"I would never resent helping a friend. What's this really about?"

"Nothing. Just looking out for you," she said lightly. She released her hold and turned, yanking at the hoses that had the old washer hooked into the water system. Soon the machines were swapped out, the new one hooked up to power and water, the old one left on the curb for the brothers to pick up later. Brant couldn't figure out what had her so unsettled, but knew he had to remain calm, patient and persistent. He wouldn't stop being himself. He knew she found it difficult to need help, but soon she'd be set up to live her life as she wished once again. And he wanted her to notice that he was still here, still looking for that chance to make her smile.

"Do you have a load of laundry to try?" he asked, testing the machine's buttons.

Without a word, April disappeared with a grin. She returned with a basket heaped with colors.

As she dumped clothing into the machine, she looked as giddy as she had when Carmichael had presented her with her first rodeo horse, Cookies. She'd been thirteen, and over the moon, she and the horse becoming fast friends.

Brant still remembered the way she'd looked that day. Maybe because that was when he'd started to see her as more than just a pesky girl stuck on their ranch who was too eager to please his annoying, overconfident older brother.

A few colorful garments landed near his feet, and Brant bent to pick them up, hesitating when he realized the scrap on his left boot was red satin underwear. He scooped it up along with a peach-tinted bra, clearing his throat as he tossed them into the machine. Apparently April didn't hand-wash her delicates like the label suggested you should, but rather subjected them to the abuse of regular washing. She never had struck him as the type to fuss over "shoulds." 'He'd also never imagined her undergarments, but if he had, they likely would've been practical and white. Not these playful, bright, sexy and revealing items that would be fun to remove from her...

It was time to think about something else.

April started the cycle and did a little dance when the sound of pouring water began.

"I am so happy I could kiss you." She turned to him in the alcove, her hands flat against his chest.

That was all the invitation he needed.

APRIL'S EYES automatically drifted shut as Brant's lips lowered to hers. She'd been waiting for this moment since their last kiss on Christmas Day.

"And here we are again," she whispered as she closed the fraction of an inch between them, placing her mouth on his. Her earlier fears about getting involved were forgotten as his stubble gently brushed her cheek and lips.

Her hands were on his chest, and she allowed them to glide up to his neck, cradling his ears as though needing to prevent him from escaping. Her fingers splayed in his soft hair, the warmth of his body pressing into hers. Everything about him felt right. His kiss was like a shelter. Safe to get lost in. She didn't have to worry about it changing to something dangerous or demanding. She could let go, vanquish her fears and be in this moment. Here, she was cared for and protected.

It was something she could get used to.

Brant broke the kiss.

"Why did you do that?" she murmured.

"Because here we are again," he said gently, placing another light peck against her lips. He was addicting, offering something she hadn't realized she'd been craving. She tightened her hold.

"Why don't we want to be here again?" She pulled his willing lips to hers again, opening her mouth to deepen the kiss. He groaned, giving her a sense of power. He had backed her against the washing machine as they kissed, but she didn't feel trapped. She felt wanted and needed.

This, right here in Brant's arms, was where she belonged.

But somewhere in the back of her mind there was an argument she wanted to ignore. Something about good things turning to bad. About their lives not being perfectly timed.

Yet Donna had said the right person made everything work out, and that's how April felt with Brant. Like everything was going to be okay.

He was the right man, and that meant this could work.

His hands ran down her sides, then cupped her bottom as he brought her closer. She sighed into his mouth, wishing every kiss on earth could be like this one. She'd never need anything ever again. No oxygen, no food, nothing but Brant and a feeling of being safe and sound.

"I always want to be here," Brant said.

"Hmm?" she murmured, turning her mouth away to speak, while his lips trailed down her neck, causing her to shiver in anticipation.

"But you said you're not ready. Did you change your mind?"

April opened her eyes. She inhaled sharply, her hands against Brant's powerful chest. He was already stepping away to give her space before she could flex her wrists or ask for what she needed.

He said nothing, didn't apologize, didn't ask if she was okay.

He was Brant. He just knew.

And because he knew, he probably recognized just how dangerous she was feeling. How she was willing to renege on those important promises she'd made to herself only that morning. How she wanted to keep diving in, even though a part of her was scared that doing so would ruin everything.

BRANT WANTED to close the physical distance he'd put between himself and April. He wanted to ignore the fact that she was breathing hard, hesitance shadowing her eyes. She needed a moment. He knew he was plucking at the pieces of her already broken resolve, and he didn't want to hate himself later. But that kiss had been hotter and longer, making their Christmas kisses seem sweet and innocent by comparison.

April was biting her bottom lip, her hands braced on the washing machine churning behind her as though that might hold her back from either strangling him or kissing him. When she looked up at him again he saw fire, passion and fear.

He liked the first two. The third one was the dragon he had to slay in order to get the princess. Or in his case, the former rodeo queen.

About a million thoughts ran through Brant's head, his brain patiently repeating that he needed to say something. Anything. The only problem was that every thought parading around in his mind right now didn't seem appropriate.

"I thought about it, April," he said at last. "I thought about it long and hard. Yeah, I might be rescuing you. But even if you didn't need any help right now? This is still the exact same place you'd find me."

April didn't speak, her chest expanding.

"The truth is," he continued, "you wouldn't play along, letting me pretend this heat between us was real because you felt grateful or obligated, or feared I'd take it all away. You're tougher than any game or guilt trip, and if you ever felt obligated to me, you'd tell me to drive off a cliff."

A slight smile played at her lips.

Truth.

He shifted his weight, taking up some of the space between them. "You can't fake the heat we have. You can't fake the way we feel when we look at each other, or when we touch. Why wait? Why give up time we could have together?"

Her lip was still caught between her teeth, her gaze on his boots.

He placed his hands over hers on the washing machine, boxing her in. She straightened, her surprise clear. How did she keep that sweet sunshine smell under the hint of veterinary clinic medicine that clung to her bright blue blouse?

"We've known each other almost our entire lives, and when have we ever fought?" He let that idea soak in while he allowed his gaze to trail over her face, taking in the way her cheeks rounded, then curved down to her generous pink lips, and her stubborn chin jutting out at him.

Her left shoulder dropped, the narrow bit of space between their mouths not seeming to faze her. Her fingers were warm under his, the machine's cold metal a contrast.

"Just because we don't fight doesn't mean something would work between us right now," she said, her voice low.

"You're scared?"

She nodded, her eyes damp.

"I'm not."

Her eyes were big, her lips clamped together. She looked pained, but she was listening despite her fears.

"Know why? We've both had crash-and-burn relationships. And yeah, that should make us scared. But I'm not, because if I'd been with the right person, it would have worked out. That person can calm us in anger and settle us when the urge comes to bolt." He softened his voice even further. "When you're with the right person, their love helps you overcome your worst fears."

Her inhale was shuddery, her eyes suddenly damp.

"You've kept me in your life longer than any other man. You've—"

"Stop." April raised a trembling hand, yanking it out from under his. "I know we're good together. I *know* that. I just don't want to hurt you, Brant, and I want to be… *more.*"

"More? More than what?"

"I want to be able to offer you more than coupons for Christmas."

"Money doesn't matter to me, April." She lowered her gaze, and he realized it was about pride and a feeling of self-sufficiency. He barely held his frustration in check. "I know how strong you are."

"I don't feel strong."

"Let me be your rock."

She laughed, the sound shuddery. "You already are."

He smiled, softening his voice to just above a whisper. "You can tell me to wait, and I will. But I'm never going to leave you."

He could see the change in her eyes. The desire to believe him, to let go and fall into what they were developing between them.

"Want to know what I know?" he asked. "I know this." He ate the minuscule distance between them again, his hips against hers as he clasped his hands on either side of her mouth, drawing her in for a long, hot kiss that left her trembling.

"There will be no denying that." He stared into her eyes for a long beat before turning and marching out of her house.

APRIL PROPPED herself against the humming washing machine for several minutes after Brant left. She exhaled, gripping the neckline of her shirt and pulled it in and out a few times to cool herself down.

That entire exchange had been hot.

That all-new side of Brant Wylder had been possibly the sexiest thing she'd ever experienced. He was sweet and gentle, yet willing to hold his ground and push her. Demanding. Sweet. Gentle. Firm.

She'd never had a man tell her he'd wait for her. They had always been my-way-now-or-hit-the-highway, chickie.

And Brant had meant it, too.

But could *she* handle waiting? Or would she incinerate dealing with all the heat that sizzled between them—especially with that last kiss? Maybe that was what Donna had been saying earlier, about things being different when you were with the right person. It just worked. Everything worked.

That would mean she didn't need to wait, become stronger or more independent.

Brant was already her rock, the strength behind her. But it was risky getting involved with the man who held her entire precarious life in his hands when it came to her finances.

That would clear up if Jenny truly offered her a job, and

Heath made his child-support payments. Then April wouldn't be as dependent on Brant, and everything would work out. Right?

And that could start as early as January—less than a week away.

But could she really hold her head high, jump into dating Brant and let the town brand him as a home-wrecker?

What would that do to Kurt?

Daddy Brant.

Her son would be elated to have him as part of their family.

Just like she would. Kurt would be surrounded by love, which would negate any rumors about the speed of her and Brant's relationship. The fact was, Brant helped her be a good, stable mom who thought before she reacted.

The only problem with choosing Brant would be how they'd set the rumor mill on fire, but maybe all her worries weren't nearly as big as she'd once thought.

Maybe it was time to take it slow and see where their hearts led them, ignoring the world around them and trusting that Brant's steady practical nature would keep them on the right path.

After all, he wouldn't pursue this if it was a bad idea.

4

---

*A*pril was really hoping Jenny Oliver had been serious about her job offer at Blue Tumbleweed, because she wasn't sure she could work for Brant any longer. Whenever he came into the front office of the clinic, which was several times a day, it was as though someone was tickling her spine with tiny electric fingers. At times she became so aware, to the point of distraction, that she found herself turning with a smile before she'd fully realized he was there.

In other words, she couldn't get him off her mind, and as a result had already stapled her blouse to two customer receipts today.

To make matters worse, since Brant had walked out of her house after that consuming kiss on Monday, he'd barely said a word to her. He had spent the past three days torturing her with long, hard stares full of heat.

The ball was so firmly in her court her racket arm was twitching.

No wonder he was on her mind. He was giving her space, but also making it very clear what he wanted, and the tension that brought to the relationship was becoming intolerable. Something had to give.

She needed to come up with a game plan.

As she flicked the switch to change the Call of the Wyld(er) sign from Open to Closed, those electric fingers worked their way up her back again. She turned, finding Brant at her desk, plopping into her chair.

"Going out tonight?" he asked.

"Jackie and I are heading to the Watering Hole." It was New Year's Eve, and the saloon was holding its annual party. One long night of dancing, drinking, eating unhealthy bar food, and generally having a good time and making poor decisions.

"Great, see you there."

Before April could reply, he was up and out the door, his key chain swinging idly on his index finger as he whistled his way past the front window.

If she didn't whack that ball back into his court tonight she was going to regret it.

"You'd better watch out, Wylder," she whispered as he moved out of sight. "You've forgotten who you're playing with."

April quickly finished locking up, and yelped in surprise when Robyn, Brant's upstairs tenant, popped in to do her list of light jobs.

"You scared me," April said.

"Sorry."

The expectant teen mom-to-be seemed distracted. "Are you okay?" Fearing the worst, she eyed the girl's belly, which wasn't yet showing under her bulky Sweetheart Creek cheer team sweatshirt. Robyn wasn't due until the summer, and April hoped she was well.

"Did you take a paternity test with Kurt?" the teenager blurted.

April was taken aback by the question. She shook her head. "He's Heath's. I hadn't been with Cole in months." She felt like she'd be telling that to the town long past her death. She paused, realizing the girl might want a test for herself. "Wait… Your baby might not be Blake's?" It didn't seem possible, since the devoted pair seemed as though they'd marry young and remain that way well into their eighties.

"It is," Robyn confirmed, "but my parents want one."

"They do?" Last April had heard, Robyn was emancipated.

Her eyes filled with tears. "They want to sue Blake's parents for damages."

"Damages?" April felt a wave of anger rising, and forced herself to calm down. Robyn needed a rational adult right now, not more emotion swirling around her. Her parents had kicked her out of the house last month, with Brant and his family ensuring she had proper care and shelter ever since.

Robyn couldn't speak through her tears.

"Hey, it's okay." April pulled her into a hug. "What do you need? How can I help?"

She sniffed. "I don't want to take a test."

"Does Blake want one?"

Robyn shook her head. "My parents said they'll take me back if I get one."

"Is that what you want?"

"I don't know. Everything feels so difficult, so confusing. They're my *parents*. But I don't want them to hurt Blake and his family."

April squeezed her again. "Why don't I look up the info on how to take a test, and then at least you'll have it. Information is power, right?" Her words felt empty. How could arming Robyn's parents to better lambaste Blake and his family be in any way a positive? But she understood how important family was, and being cut off from that support at such a young age, and at such a trying time, would be so incredibly difficult. April thanked her own lucky stars that she'd been surrounded by lots of loving people ready to help her do the right thing when she'd found herself unexpectedly pregnant in her twenties. "Would that help?"

Robyn nodded and pulled away, wiping her eyes. "Thank you."

"Anything you need, I'm here." She waited for Robyn to nod. "Anything. Anytime. Okay? I've been through this stuff." She gave the girl a wry smile. "I know what it can feel like. It's a lot."

Robyn nodded and smiled through her tears, and April, once assured the girl was going to be okay, hurried to pick up Kurt from day care.

By seven both April and he were fed and on their way to the Sweet Meadows Ranch, where Maria Wylder would take Kurt for a sleepover in her tiny home. She'd moved the three-hundred-square-foot house into the side yard last fall, and Kurt was enamored with sleeping in the miniature building.

One of the nice things about being in town again, after several years of being forty minutes away, was Maria. April had grown up in her kitchen, and the woman had been more of a mother figure than her own mom, who was living on a sixteenth-floor condo in Dallas. Her mother brokered large real estate deals and worked long hours, her interests nowhere close to April's or even motherhood. How she and April's father, a ranch hand who spent his evenings and paychecks on poker and beer, had ever found enough in common to have a child was beyond April.

Moving onto the ranch as a kid and becoming part of the big, bustling Wylder family had been exactly what April needed. Now, with Heath mostly absent from Kurt's life, the Wylder clan and their closeness meant something special to her in an all-new way.

As April turned down the long driveway, she noted lights on in the main ranch house, a rambling affair that had been added onto many times in its fifty years. Maria was often there, so April parked between the matriarch's restored Mustang and Brant's veterinarian truck out front. Then she and Kurt headed for the door, after shushing Levi's dog, Lupe, Brant's dog, Dodge, Myles's dog, Buckey, and Maria's new dog, Bingo.

"I want a dog!" Kurt laughed, holding Buckey in a loose head-lock as the black animal happily licked hiss face.

"I'm sure Brant will find one for us someday soon." She'd asked him to stay on the lookout for a suitable pet, not quite sure how she'd pay for it, seeing as Heath was still holding out with variations of his I'll-see-Kurt-if-you-go-on-a-date-with-me all-or-nothing offers. He'd made several separate ones now, and it was driving her nuts.

She was going to have to ask her lawyer to speak to him about their custody agreement, as well as payments. She loved having Kurt more than her share, but Heath's payments should reflect the uneven distribution of care. As far as she was concerned, if he wanted to play games, he could play them with the lawyers. Although maybe she'd better get her big-eater of a horse off his property. Otherwise she might not have much of a leg to stand on when it came to arguing about money, since, technically, he was currently boarding Cookies.

Before April could hit the bell, the door opened and Bingo raced inside with a joyful bark. April had been bracing herself to see Brant, and to act normal, but it was Cole who stood there.

"Hey, hey," he said. "Happy New Year's Eve."

"Hey." April tightened her coat around her. "Is your mom here? Or is she at her place?"

"Thought you might be here to see Brant. I heard rumors about you two."

April rolled her eyes and sighed.

"Brant's staying with Carmichael. He gave me his room."

"That's nice." Her body heated at the mention of him, and she tried to contain her smile. "Your mom's babysitting Kurt so I can go out with Jackie."

"Jackie, huh? How's she doing?"

"Fine. Is Maria here?"

She was planning to put some subtle moves on Brant tonight, and that meant she needed to *not* see him here. She'd squeezed herself into a dress that was a bit too small, and she had to admit it looked fabulous despite its tightness. She wanted to watch Brant's eyes trace her figure in that way of his that made her proud of her new curves. She'd been able to catch eyes when she'd been younger and thinner, but this was different. Her body seemed to hold a different power and strength, and she'd poured herself into this dress to... Well, she wasn't sure yet. But she didn't want him to see her here, as he might feel he had to hide the effect her dress had on him from his family. And she wanted to see it all, unmasked.

Tonight was about courage, new beginnings, and showing him she was ready to move past her fears and start something slow.

"Big thing at the Watering Hole, hmm?" Cole ran a hand through his hair. He seemed to be waking up more. She used to find her ex-boyfriend's sleepy-eyed gaze sexy, like an animal she could tame, unlike wide-awake Cole. Currently, she found his lack of alertness tried her patience.

He rubbed an eye, and she narrowed her attention. Wait. Cole Wylder had been taking a nap at seven o'clock on New Year's Eve? Unheard of. Usually he had already primed himself with a few beers by now, preparing for an adventure.

"You're not going out?" April asked.

"I might." He gave a casual shrug, leaning against the partially open door as if he had all the time in the world.

"There's my little cowboy!" Maria said, appearing from the office down the hall, where April knew she'd set up a small area for painting miniature canvases. She hurried toward them, tugging the smock she'd been wearing over her head, then stretching out her arms to Kurt. Cole had opened the door all the way, and Kurt ran straight to her, receiving a hug that warmed April's heart.

"Cole, let April in and close the door. It's cold out there tonight."

He gave a sheepish grimace. "Sorry. Just woke up."

"I have Kurt's overnight bag here," April said, putting it down inside the door. "His stuffed animal from Carmichael is in it." The seventy-nine-year-old had won a purple unicorn at the library fundraiser fair in early November and given it to Kurt. The toy and the kid had barely been separated since.

"Okay. Have fun with Jackie tonight," Maria said, coming over to give April a hug, Cole silently watching the exchange. "We're going to bake cookies, then eat a few, watch a movie, and try to stay up until midnight."

Kurt did a little dance of excitement.

"Midnight?" April exclaimed, as though it was an unbelievable idea for her four-year-old. She widened her eyes at Kurt and he giggled.

"You're not supposed to know, Mom. It's a secret!"

"I'll pretend I never heard it then?" April suggested, and he nodded. To Maria she said, "I'll pick him up around noon tomorrow? Or would you like me to come sooner?"

"Noon's fine. If you want, can you come for lunch?"

"That would be nice."

"Brant was saying some payments haven't come through for you?" Maria gave Kurt a pointed glance, obviously referring to Heath and child support. "If you need anything, you let me know, okay? My pantry's always fully stocked and there are always extra chairs at our table."

April bit her lips, pushing back the swell of gratitude. She nodded, unable to speak.

Maria patted her arm, then opened the door for her. "It won't be long until everything is all straightened out and back to normal for you. Hang in there."

"Do you need tickets at the Watering Hole tonight?" Cole asked, as April stepped onto the porch.

She shook her head. She'd be nursing one beer all night, making it a cheap night out.

She got in her vehicle, disappointed that she hadn't seen Brant, even though she hadn't wanted to. She lowered her forehead to the steering wheel for a moment, kicking herself for not asking Maria if she could board Cookies in her stable. However, the woman was already doing so much for her. It felt wrong to ask for more, especially when April knew she'd never say no. Maybe Ryan's girlfriend, Carly, had room in her stable next door, and April could find enough spare cash in her next paycheck to cut a deal.

Or maybe it was time to sell Cookies. The problem was, selling the horse Carmichael had given her when she was thirteen felt like selling her best friend. Cookies was an old fellow now, still strong but in his twenties, and he deserved a lovely retirement, not abandonment.

Determined to move her thoughts away from her horse guilt, she lifted her head from the steering wheel and thought about Brant. She didn't have an official plan for tonight, just knew she wanted to catch his attention. Even though she already had it.

She sighed.

Okay, so besides the dress, she had no actual plan.

She was hoping that tonight would give her the strength to build an argument so strong she'd have no choice but to give in to her belief that Brant Wylder was absolutely the perfect man for her and that she should do something about it.

Rather immediately.

BRANT HAD BEEN TORTURING himself ever since that hot moment when he'd all but bent April over the washing machine in her little laundry nook and consumed her mouth with his own.

His thoughts were locked in a circle, all of them revolving around one thing, one woman, one idea, one desire.

He wanted to have April MacFarlane as his, and being patient was taking a toll on him. She needed some time and space to heal, and he needed to cool his jets. Something he'd once excelled at.

But the anticipation and tension building between them was well past torturous. How much time did a woman need? He'd seen the way she looked at him. She didn't want to wait, either.

He straightened his white cowboy hat and smoothed the front of his button-up shirt. He'd chosen a plain, rectangular belt buckle, dark wash jeans and a comfortable pair of brown cowboy boots he could dance in all night. Parking on Main Street, he left his black insulated vest in the truck, and walked down to the Watering Hole.

The place was hopping for nine o'clock, with people milling about outside the bar, smoking and laughing, and music pouring out into the air every time someone came or went. The old-style swinging doors that local dogs ducked under had been latched to the inner full-length doors to keep out the December cold.

Brant paused to pet Rusty, a dog who'd adopted the saloon and its owners due to his love of their day-old cheese bread.

"Busy in there tonight, pal. You might have to wait until tomorrow to get your treats."

The brown and white mutt fell into step behind him, his tail wagging hopefully. At the doors, Brant gave a shake of his head and Rusty sat with a plaintive whine.

"Sorry, buddy."

Inside, the saloon was warm, with bodies packed wall to wall. Those on the raised platform with the pool tables at the back barely had enough space to take their shot.

Finding April should be difficult in the moving crowd and dim lighting, but his gaze locked on her immediately. She was wearing a blue dress that should be illegal. The way it hugged her body was practically indecent, showing every curve that had filled out with motherhood. So many sexy curves.

Brant swallowed hard, trying to act casual as an internal homing beacon urged him to walk directly to her. Instead, he headed toward the bar, where people were packed four deep, waving to the bartenders to take their order.

Daisy-Mae Ray, one of Myles's ex-girlfriends, came up, holding a tray above the throng of people. "What can I get you, hon?"

"You're working here again?" Brant asked. She hadn't in years.

She gave him a dazzling grin and a little shimmy, showing off her tied-up, button-up shirt that had probably already been two sizes too small when she was a teen, and her short, cut-off jeans. Like the rest of the staff, she was wearing black boots and a black cowboy hat. She looked like she could be in a beer commercial or a country and western music video.

"Best tipping night of the year," she drawled.

"I'll bet." He ordered a beer.

"You better order two. It might be a while before I can get back around to you."

Behind him Brant heard someone say with exasperation, "Quit taking more orders and bring me my drinks, Daisy-Mae."

"Start tipping better and I'll make you a priority, sweetie," she said, blowing the man a kiss.

The guy's grumpy face softened, and Brant chuckled. He placed a few bills in the glass on Daisy-Mae's tray, paying her in advance. "I'll take two of whatever light beer you have on tap."

"Myles and Karen are over by the band with Levi and Laura, if you're looking for them," she said. "And if you're looking for April, she's the one beating off admirers in the center of the room."

Brant pivoted to check her out. There was a man at her table now, standing over her, leaning in too close.

"Since you broke up her marriage, you'd better get in there and make sure it wasn't all for nothin," Daisy-Mae advised.

"I didn't break up her marriage." Brant made a point of turning back to face her, very aware that April was more than capable of taking care of a drunk interloper. In fact, so were Jackie, Jenny and Carly, who were sharing her table.

"So you didn't come along looking like the sexiest thing, ready to save her from her marriage doldrums?" Daisy-Mae ran a finger across Brant's collarbone before she shimmied off with a sly smile.

"Not intentionally," he said absently, his urge to liberate April strengthening as he glanced over his shoulder. The man was smiling hopefully. Brant wanted to smear the look right off his face.

Daisy-Mae weaved her way behind the bar and Brant considered his next move. He didn't want to press in on April, as a few kisses didn't give him the right to beat away other men. He wanted it to, though. He wanted a lot more than a few kisses with her, too.

That would be rescuing her, though, wouldn't it? And she'd made it clear she didn't want that.

He cursed softly under his breath, feeling torn.

Wade Ross, a man down on his luck, staggered by, stumbling into Brant. He propped the man back on his feet and glanced April's way again. The interloper was gone. Brant's jaw loosened.

Daisy-Mae appeared moments later, quickly handing him two beers before disappearing into a throng of people to deliver the rest of the drinks on her tray.

Someone jostled Brant's elbow. It was his brother Ryan, who took Brant's extra beer with a thanks. He clinked the glass against Brant's.

"Seen Carly?" Ryan asked.

"Middle of the room with April, Jenny and Jackie."

"How long have you been here?"

"Maybe five minutes?"

"And already have a drink and found the girls?"

Brant shrugged.

"Well? What are you doing standing over here?" Ryan began weaving his way toward the table, Brant following. The place was packed, the tables and chairs so close together it was an ordeal to get to the women.

As they arrived at the table, Jenny Oliver was saying to April, loudly enough to be heard over the music, "I'm serious. I'm going to have an opening in about a week—maybe two—at Blue Tumbleweed. You'll get discounts on all the clothes. So it doesn't matter if things fit or not, you just buy more."

"Are you trying to poach my best employee?" Brant said with a frown. He squeezed into a tight, standing-room-only spot with his brother, with chairs from the next table pressed up behind them.

April blushed, her gaze lingering on him, clearly noticing details in a way that left Brant pleased he'd taken some care with his outfit. He stroked his chin and realized he'd forgotten to shave, then let out a sigh. He wasn't used to trying to impress a woman.

"As a matter of fact, I am." Jenny beamed up at him, her cheeks flushed from the girlie drink set in front of her. The poor gal always turned pink after a bit of alcohol.

Brant struggled to focus on what they'd been talking about. A job. Poaching April.

Not on his life.

"Well, I wish you'd stop."

"I think it's smart."

"Hi, Brant." Violet Granger, sitting at the table behind him, caught his attention. She turned her chair sideways, then scooted her butt forward, leaving a small space behind her. "We can share."

"You sure?" he asked. The tables were close enough that they could each perch on the chair and be part of their own table's conversations. She gave him a shy smile and nodded.

Brant glanced at April, hoping to receive a similar offer, but she was too busy glaring at Violet. So he sat down gingerly, keeping his legs out to support him, forearms across his thighs.

"Why is it smart?" Ryan was asking. He'd extended his free hand to Carly and pointed his feet toward the dance floor.

"Because then he won't have to fire her," Jackie stated.

"What?" April protested. She'd been glowering at the thin space between Brant and Violet and now aimed her glare at Jackie.

"Why would I fire her?" Brant asked.

"It's obviously a conflict of interest if you're crushing on your boss," Jackie said with a laugh. Ryan's eyes darted to Brant, smirking as he headed off to dance with Carly.

Brant slipped off Violet's chair with another thanks, and onto Carly's before someone could sweep it away.

"I'm not crushing," April said.

"Fine, fine. In love with him then. Although couples often work together around here. They usually get married first, though." Jackie lifted her brows meaningfully and Jenny laughed.

April rolled her eyes and Brant took a sip of his beer, wondering how he could extract April from her friends to tell her how sexy she looked in that dress, and how he hoped she'd never leave his clinic.

"You know what day it is," Jackie said, with special emphasis to ensure she had everyone's attention.

"December 31," April said in a dry tone.

"It's the day Old Man Lovely marries a couple from Sweetheart Creek." Jackie smiled and leaned back, her eyes flicking to Brant's, sending shivers down his spine. "I wonder who it will be this year?"

"Old Man Lovely is marrying Delia and Joey tonight," April stated. "That's what I heard. Not anyone at this table." She glanced at Brant and he nodded.

Jackie waved her hand. "You guys are way too chicken for something like that, anyway."

"It's called being civil, rational beings," April said indignantly, knowing her friend was trying to get under her skin.

Truthfully, she didn't want to think about eloping with Brant. It was too tempting to release the fire that was building inside her and claim the man as hers once and for all. Way too tempting.

But marriage? That was extreme.

"You're so tame these days," Jenny teased. She leaned closer. "But you know, it *would* stop some of the rumors."

And it would also shut down Heath's stupid games, as well as her fears that Brant was interested in her only because she needed his help. Yes, she'd already worked the angles in the past several seconds.

"New topic." April put her beer to her lips, knowing that she'd be unable to focus on anything but Brant and Old Man Lovely's chapel now. Especially since, despite the crush of people in the Watering Hole, April could smell Brant's aftershave as he sat beside her in Carly's chair. He looked so handsome, and it was all she could do not to study his forearms as he rolled up his sleeves in the thick heat of the packed saloon.

She was definitely crushing on her boss. And she would love to put a stop to all the rumors floating around her, and settle into a new life without all this uncertainty. It would be good for her, for Kurt, and for Brant, too.

"How's your drink?" he asked, gesturing to the bottle in front of her.

"Still good, thanks," she said, lifting it to take another sip. She'd never had issues keeping up a conversation with Brant, but at the moment she felt tongue-tied, the silence awkward. She'd spent so much time thinking about him over the past few days, wondering, waiting. And from the time she'd arrived, shortly after seven, she'd been scanning the Watering Hole for him. Now he was here, and she didn't know what to do with him.

She'd thought a grand plan would come to mind when she saw him, but beyond wearing a tight dress, she had nothing.

She wanted to be with him. Wanted to jump over the awkward uncertainty of a new relationship and right into the happily ever after.

"Do you have tomorrow off?" she asked Jackie, despite knowing the answer. Brant was watching her, and she felt unfocused, unsettled. Distracted. She grew hot under his gaze, which kept tracking her body like it was something he wanted to sample.

"Do you need me to leave so you two can make out?" Jackie asked, hands on the table as though ready to push away.

April laughed too loudly.

Brant took another sip of his beer, as if mulling over the offer. Then he set down his glass and slid his right arm along the back of April's chair as he leaned closer. Her body prickled with awareness.

"Whatever makes you comfortable," he said to Jackie, his voice a deep rumble.

April laughed at his teasing. There was no way he'd kiss her here. Unless maybe it was midnight and they were on the dance floor.

She turned to check Brant's expression and found his lips connecting with hers. She didn't kiss back at first, frozen in surprise until he deepened the kiss. He tasted of hops, and his body was warm and firm. She snuggled closer, stroking the rough stubble on his jaw with her fingers.

For a moment she forgot where she was, until he broke the kiss.

She felt dazed.

"Look at that, and it's not even midnight yet," Jackie said, dusting her hands together. "My work here is done."

"I'm sure it's midnight somewhere," Brant said, his eyes lingering on April's lips.

"Rumor is Old Man Lovely stays in his little chapel on the hill until two in the morning," Jenny said cheerily, "waiting for a taker."

"We forgot to say Happy New Year before we kissed," April said to Brant, shifting in her seat so she could slide her hands over his shoulders and into the hair at the nape of his neck, just under his cowboy hat. She could kiss this man all day.

"Happy New Year," he murmured between kisses. "Is that new perfume?"

"It's cinnamon. I sprinkled it on our squash so Kurt would eat it at suppertime."

"Well, it's making me hungry." Brant tightened his arms around her and she felt a surge of excitement at the potential of his embrace.

"There aren't any more seats," she heard Jackie say loudly, her tone flirty. "But you can share with me."

April broke the kiss, glancing over her shoulder. Jenny and her chair were gone and Cole was standing in that spot, shifting awkwardly. Before she could react, Brant had clasped her hand and was pulling her onto the dance floor with a command to Cole, "Save our seats."

Without waiting for confirmation from his brother, Brant tugged her into the throng of moving bodies, holding her close. One thing she loved about country songs was that all the dances involved holding your partner. The musical genre had definitely gotten that right.

With one hand on Brant's shoulder and the other tucked in his grasp, April allowed him to lead her around the dance floor. She did her best not to check on their table to see what Jackie and Cole were up to.

Unable to resist, she finally took a peek. Cole was leaning back in his chair, looking lost, while Jackie's smile seemed too bright and tight. That woman needed to find her courage and go for it.

The same could be said about herself.

April returned her focus to Brant, whose warm smile widened when she made eye contact. Suddenly she felt as though she was standing too close, the expectations and desires too much for her to handle. There was so much potential. What if she messed up? She focused on breathing, on looking away and remaining cool.

All she could think about was the feel of his lips on hers.

"What was that back there?" she asked, referring to the kiss.

"You didn't want to dance?" Brant replied.

"You know what I mean."

"Opportunity knocked."

"And so you opened the door?"

He grinned.

They were going to start more rumors, but she was so tired of worrying about what other people thought. Brant was a wonderful man, and everyone in town knew that. He hadn't broken up her marriage, but maybe it hadn't been right to be such good friends with a man who wasn't your husband. Maybe that was why Heath had signed their divorce papers so quickly; he had seen that April and he didn't have that closeness. But the games? Was his pride taking a hit with the gossip going around about her and Brant?

She shook off her thoughts. She was in Brant's arms, ready for a new beginning.

"How late are you staying tonight?" she asked him.

"Not sure. You?"

She shrugged, wishing it was already midnight, so they'd have an excuse to kiss again without drawing excessive attention.

"Earlier you made it sound as though you had something planned for me."

"I did?" Brant's steps slowed, and she stumbled into him. He held her close until they regained their footing. And even then he continued to hold her tight.

He had a five o'clock shadow, no doubt an animal emergency having prevented him from shaving before coming out for New Year's Eve. Or maybe he just knew what a turn-on it was and had opted to skip the razor.

"I guess it was just a feeling."

"You wanted another surprise?"

"Maybe."

"The kiss didn't surprise you?"

"Maybe." She shrugged, feeling shy.

"You want more surprises?"

"I'm greedy that way."

"What are you greedy for?"

"What are you offering?"

His lips lowered, until his mouth just about on hers. "Everything you'd like."

This felt like a fantasy.

"You're forgetting something important, April MacFarlane." He'd pulled her body close to his, her thin, tight dress doing little to prevent his appetizing heat from warming her soul.

"What's that?" she asked breathlessly, barely daring to consider how dangerous this bold side of sweet Brant made her feel.

"I know you better than anyone else."

"Do you?"

"And I know exactly what you need."

"And what do I need?"

His lips landed on hers, hard, hot and demanding. She wrapped her arms around his neck as they swayed in the middle of the dance floor.

5

Brant continued to kiss April on the dance floor, ignoring the catcalls that echoed around them. Anyone who had a problem could speak to him. He had waited a long time for April, and tonight he wasn't waiting any longer.

"Can I cut in?" a deep voice asked, as soon as they paused for a breath. They had been locked together, dancing long forgotten.

Brant turned toward the man, his focus hazy. He wanted to get out of here with April. They weren't paying attention to the outside world, anyway, and the interruptions were very unwelcome.

"No," April said firmly, causing Brant to focus on the situation. Her ex-husband, Heath, was facing them with a scowl.

"I'd like a second chance."

"No."

Brant's hands were still around April's waist, and he instinctively swung her to his side.

"I'm not falling for the fake boyfriend thing." Heath gestured to Brant.

"He's not a fake boyfriend!" April called over Brant's shoulder.

Seeing this conversation wouldn't head anywhere good, Brant

pivoted, planning to steer himself and April back to the safety of their table. As soon as he turned away from Heath he realized his mistake.

A powerful hand used to handling rodeo livestock clamped onto his shoulder and spun him around.

Having grown up with four brothers, Brant trusted his instincts and ducked. Heath's fist whizzed past his forehead, readjusting his hat, which was perched on the back of his head because of April's wandering hands during that searing kiss. Brant grabbed it with one hand to keep it from tumbling to the sticky floor, and pushed April behind him with the other. As he straightened, another punch came his way, this one a right hook to his ribs. He curved away from the blow, exhaling and avoiding the worst of the impact.

The music was still pumping through the warm saloon, but people had crushed together to create a ring of space around the fighting duo. Over the roaring in Brant's ears, he heard April yelling at her ex.

Brant kept his focus on Heath, barely aware of the men who flanked his sides, two on each side. His brothers.

The five of them were certainly going to hear about this from their mother in the morning, if not sooner.

"She's mine, you interloper," Heath growled, his words slurring. Brant exhaled. He'd had a feeling this would happen, especially getting involved with April so soon after the breakup. Heath would assume it was a game, or that the two of them had stepped out behind his back. He might not consider that it was only about April and her happiness.

Brant kept his mouth shut, not wanting to escalate the situation and humiliate her. He watched Heath's moves, ready to block or swing if need be.

"He didn't steal me!" April yelled from behind Brant.

"He's been trying to steal you for years, but you're too dumb to see it!" Heath retorted.

"Hey, now," Brant said, struggling for calm. Then his hackles rose again when Cole positioned himself slightly in front of him.

"Their relationship isn't your business," his brother said firmly.

"Yeah?" Heath replied with a sneer. "Maybe I should scare this Wylder off, too."

Brant growled at Cole and pulled him back. He didn't need his brother coming to blows with Heath like they had the night before Cole left town. He had disappeared with a shiner, a swollen lip and his truck, leaving behind plenty of speculation.

Brant also didn't need his brother whisking in and saving April like he used to when bars got rowdy during their rodeo days.

"I've got this," he said, and Cole backed off, his stance making it clear he was still ready for a fight.

"But Cole's right. Who April dates isn't your business," Brant declared.

"You made your life my business when you gave April a house so she could leave me." Heath jabbed a finger in Brant's direction. "We were working things out. Her beloved horse is still at my place. That means something, you know. She still has one foot in the door." He moved close, and his breath was hot like his anger. "*My* door."

Brant inhaled slowly, trying to reject the possible kernel of truth in Heath's words. April did have a tough time letting go. First with Cole, always going back for another round. Now with Heath. She'd struggled to pull the pin on their marriage for almost two years, and Brant feared that for Kurt's sake she really might try to patch things up, even though she'd never truly loved the man.

"Leaving Cookies at the farm doesn't mean a thing," April said. "You refused to work on our relationship. Nothing ever changed. You gave me nothing but lip service for almost five years."

"If you loved me, you wouldn't need to change me." Heath focused back on Brant. "You told her to leave. You were always there, then hiring her some lawyers, and showing up at the custody hearing. Now you're telling her to ask for money." Heath's posture straightened, as if he planned to chest-bump Brant right out of the saloon. "You need to back out of our business."

Heath stepped forward to shove Brant, who sidestepped, leaving the man stumbling into space. Brant reached out and righted him before he could fall against April.

A wall of Wylders protected her from the fray, but she pushed her way through to glare at her ex as if she wanted to rip the brown curls from his head. "Be a dad to your son or increase your child-support payments."

"How am I supposed to do that? I'm on the road trying to make a living. I don't see you working as hard as I am. You're out partying with this home-wrecker."

Brant heard someone behind Heath give a grunt of agreement.

"She's working hard so she can afford to feed and clothe your growing son," Brant said, his fury building. "You agreed to your current custody and support arrangement. Be a man and honor it."

"Why don't you just marry her so I can stop paying through the nose?"

"Maybe I will," Brant said, squaring off, a sense of calm cooling him.

"I don't recommend eloping," Ryan said, his voice flat. The warning was heard by all. This was Old Man Lovely's night to marry two people who were operating on a whim.

Brant knew it wouldn't be him and April.

But there were a lot of reasons why it should be.

Heath rushed forward and Brant's brothers stepped together to block him before he could reach Brant.

"Get her out of here," Myles said, as they pinned Heath in place. Brant took April by the elbow, turning them away from the wrestling match.

He hated to back out of a fight and run, but Myles was right. April didn't need to be here, especially not if the humiliating scene erupted into something even bigger. She needed peace and the ability to move on with her life, not more town gossip centered around her.

"Let's go," he said, and she nodded as they hustled toward the bar's front door. On the way past their table, Brant lifted April's jacket from the back of her chair. Jackie and Jenny watched with open mouths as they hurried by.

The cool December air hit them and the old light above the saloon's entry flickered, causing Brant to nearly trip over Rusty, who was sleeping on the sidewalk. The dog gave a sigh and rolled over, no doubt hoping for his usual belly rub.

"We'll take my truck," Brant said, figuring Heath was upset with him, not April. He'd leave her SUV alone if it was parked on the street, but maybe not Brant's expensive mobile veterinarian unit.

As they hurried to the vehicle, he sent his mom a quick text, giving her a heads-up that Heath was on the warpath. If he wanted to pursue his vendetta, he'd likely check the Sweet Meadows Ranch as well as April's house.

His mom replied, saying she and Kurt were at her house. In other words, if Heath ventured as far as the ranch tonight, Kurt would miss a show where his father melted down. That was good.

"Mom and Kurt aren't in the main house any longer," Brant told April.

"I'm sorry," she said, as she slipped into the passenger seat.

"There's nothing to apologize for." He started the engine, one arm over the seat back as he looked out the rear window while reversing onto Main Street.

"How are your ribs?" April asked with a wince.

The adrenaline hadn't allowed the pain to register until now. Thinking about it, Brant could feel where Heath's knuckles had connected. There would be a bruised and tender spot, but nothing as bad as if he hadn't moved or exhaled at the right time.

"They're fine."

She looked skeptical, but didn't push it. "Now what?"

Now that they'd started some fresh gossip? He wasn't sure.

Brant thought for a moment. He didn't want Heath to ruin their night, and midnight was still two hours away. But where could they go and what could they do so they could bring in the New Year together?

"Swimming hole?" he suggested. As teenagers, they'd slipped out in the middle of the night for a dip sometimes. That was during the full heat of a Texas summer, not on a December night that was threatening frost. But if they parked on the bluffs, they could watch the town's midnight fireworks and likely avoid seeing anyone else.

"I am not swimming in this weather," April said with a shaky laugh.

"We could watch the fireworks from there," Brant explained as he drove past the outdoor swimming pool and only motel, heading out of town.

"Romantic evening," she said with a watery smile.

"I'm full of surprises like that." He glanced over, judging whether a romantic spot would be okay. She was studying her hands, her glance darting to the side mirror every so often as though she expected Heath to pursue them. Brant knew his brothers would keep her ex occupied until he'd cooled down, or at least until they figured Brant and April had enough of a head start.

"Are you okay?"

She sighed, silent for a long moment. "I'm trying to protect you, you know."

Brant chuckled. "I thought that was what I was doing. Protecting *you*."

She shifted to watch him in the dashboard's glow. "I don't want the choices I make to ruin the way people see you." Her tone was sincere, full of worry, making Brant's heart ache.

"You won't." He slowed the truck, turned onto a gravel road, then glanced in the rearview mirror, on the lookout for headlights following them. It grew dark behind them as the town disappeared in the distance. The truck bumped and hummed, while bits of gravel hit the undercarriage with pinging sounds.

As they rounded a bend, they spied a miniature white chapel on the hill, its windows lit up. Was someone up there right now, becoming Sweetheart Creek's couple of the year as they were wed by Old Man Lovely? Or was the man still waiting? In all his sixty-three years of doing this, not a single New Year had been missed.

As they passed the illuminated chapel Brant noted there were no vehicles parked nearby. Grant Lovely was still waiting.

"But the friends-to-lovers thing?" April asked, her brow furrowed as she turned back around, after watching the chapel retreat from view. "What happens if it doesn't last? You lose your best friend."

Brant was silent for a long moment, allowing himself to envision the friends-to-lovers part, and she let out a frustrated huff. "Brant?"

"Sorry, my mind stopped working when you said 'lovers.'"

"You're such a guy."

"I thought you found that attractive."

She smiled, shaking her head. "Is it possible to be on the rebound even though Heath and I were never really crazy in love?"

"I've never really subscribed to the rebound idea."

"What if I'm unable to maintain healthy relationships?"

"Who said that?"

"My past."

Brant mulled that over. "I'm not a volatile man, April. The last two guys you were involved with could get a little testy."

"So you're blaming them?" She shifted, and he knew he had her attention. "Even though I'm the common denominator?"

"Have they been able to keep relationships with other women?"

April's nose scrunched as she thought that over.

"You're not the same wild child you used to be," Brant said. "You've settled your demons."

"What if they're just in hibernation?" There was a lightness to her voice. She wasn't quite teasing him, but was getting close, her worries and insecurities ebbing like the day's heat after the sun set. She seemed ready to let go of what was haunting her, make a shift.

"They could be," he acknowledged, turning down the ragged dirt trail that led to the swimming hole. It was almost faster to walk from town than to drive, as you could take shortcuts through yards and meadows.

"For real, I could be on the rebound." Her tone became thoughtful. "Except mostly I just feel relief."

It wasn't the first time she'd expressed that to him. Originally, she'd said she felt as though she was in the quiet period after a storm, the stillness after a shock. When she'd first left Heath, she would often chew on her lower lip, doubts clearly gnawing at her. But Brant had noticed that since then, every time Heath misbehaved, whether it was yelling at her in the lawyers' offices, calling her out in court or failing to live up to their agreements, it seemed to steel her resolve to leave him behind. And each time, she seemed to grow lighter, her spine straightening, more of her old spark returning.

Her leaving Cookies at his place was unexpected, though. She'd said she would find somewhere for her horse when Brant had helped her and Kurt move out five weeks ago.

He rubbed his chin. Had it been only five? Things had moved so quickly it felt like longer than that.

,"You know what I want for the New Year?" she asked.

"What's that?"

"I want something certain and settled," she declared. "All this indecision and pussyfooting around everyone and our relationship is driving me nuts. Why should anyone else determine what we do or don't do?"

Brant felt his eyebrows shoot up. Her firmness over settling the uncertainty was new. He angled his truck to face the upcoming fireworks show over the town, then shut off the engine.

"So we should risk it, and get serious then?" he asked, not daring to hope that the answer might be yes. He undid his seat belt and shifted to face her.

Her bottom lip was tucked under her top teeth, her eyes large. She had an idea. He could see it in her expression, something fun and wild and fully April MacFarlane.

"Good things happen?" she asked.

He let out a huff of air, thinking that yeah, maybe good things were going to happen as a result of tonight's fight in the saloon. But for the life of him, he couldn't predict exactly what.

"Here we are again?" April quirked her lips. Her tone was lighter than it had been in days and it reminded him of their youth, of trail rides after rainstorms, when they'd go venturing out to see what had changed on the landscape. She'd been excited any time the creek flooded or a tree was downed.

Brant had angled his knees toward April, his arm over the back of the seat. He gently caressed her cheek. It was so soft, and touching it calmed a part of him. Her lashes lowered as she relaxed into the caress.

Again, the change within her took him by surprise. He wasn't certain what it was about, only knew it had something to do with them and their relationship.

Smiling, he settled into the seat, into the moment. "We're still here, April," he said, his voice a deep rumble. "Right where we've always been. But we've also never *been* here before. Not like this."

She angled herself toward him, her knees pressing into his. "No?"

"No. This is different."

"How do you know?"

"Kiss me. You'll see."

"Will I?" She shifted closer, her warm cinnamon smell encompassing him.

"You'll know everything you don't already know."

"Everything?"

"Everything."

As their kiss slowly waned, and they broke apart, April knew. Finally.

She drew in a deep breath, checking herself for doubts. There were none.

She could see the answer, what she wanted to do.

"Do you want to kill a bunch of rumors?" she asked.

"I don't want to break up with you or wait even longer," Brant said, nuzzling her neck and peppering her with slow kisses that made her head spin and her thoughts scatter.

"I'm not asking you to," she said, struggling to focus. "I'm suggesting something opposite. Something that would kill the rumors around Cole, smarten up Heath and his games, protect Kurt, and let us move on with our lives by putting it in high gear."

"High gear?" He'd found a spot that made her shiver, and he gently worked the area with his lips as she crooked her neck to give him better access. They were steaming up the truck's windows as the air in the cab became cozy and warm, blocking out the chilly night that surrounded them.

Her conviction was building within her, arguments for her idea coming one after another. Excitement swelled, and Brant, sensing a change, eased back so he could check her expression. He edged back even farther, but didn't argue, just gazed at her, somehow giving her conviction more strength. If her idea was dumb, she knew he'd say no. If he didn't genuinely feel something for her, if he was just attracted to her because of the problems he could fix, he'd say so.

"I want to do something that will help me move forward and make a clean break into my new life. I want to be stable. I want to be happy. I want to leave the past behind. I know what I want, Brant."

"You've done so much in the past few weeks, April." He was looking worried, and she gave his hand a squeeze, her giddiness growing.

"I know I have, and I've built momentum toward the life I want. Now it's time to act."

"So, you'd like to date?" There was hope in his voice.

"Brant," she said soberly, waiting for him to give her his full attention. "The lights were still on in Old Man Lovely's chapel."

He stilled, barely breathing. "What are you saying?"

Sensing his alarm gave her pause. What was she saying? That she wanted to marry Brant? Shouldn't they date first?

But why wouldn't she marry him? If they dated, this was where they'd end up. She was certain of it. He was wonderful. Stable. A lifelong friend she knew and understood. She trusted him. He was husband material. Father material. An amazing partner and pal. They never fought, and whenever their routines overlapped, it felt natural. Weren't her friends telling her that was what was vital? Not the craziness she'd had in the past?

She held Brant's hand, considering how serious she was. The more she thought about him and all he offered, and all they could be together as a couple, the more certain she became. He rocked her socks off with his kisses. And hadn't humiliated her by trying to prove his manhood in the saloon, but had stood his ground while protecting her, without hurting anyone.

And the way he made her heart beat faster when he entered any room she was in? There were no more boxes to check on her list.

Yes, marriage was rushing things a bit, but it would also hurtle them right over any uncertainty and into their happily ever after, killing all the rumors that were swirling about.

"Do you want to settle down?" she asked.

"This is big, April. Really big. You just got out of a marriage."

She nodded, then shook her head. "But that was two people trying to do the right thing. Heath and I weren't ever really in love. I'm not on the rebound, Brant." She'd never felt about Heath the way she felt about Brant.

"You think this will stop rumors, and help you with Heath?" He was rubbing his chin, looking out the windshield.

"I'm not asking you to rescue me. Don't do this unless you want to be with me."

"I want to be with you," he replied quickly. So quickly she knew it was true.

She bit her lip to prevent a huge grin from breaking free. He was considering it, really considering it.

"I want to be with *you*, Brant." She slipped her hand into his. "And this could fix a lot of things. Like you said the other day, why waste time?" It would be so much easier if they were together. Matrimony would prove he wasn't just rescuing her. And it would prove to those who felt she'd used Brant to get out of her marriage with Heath that she wanted Brant in her life for other reasons, too. It would also show them there was no Cole in her heart. Just Brant. Just the two of them and their growing feelings for each other.

And if Jenny's job at the boutique came through, she'd soon be more independent, too. She'd be able to contribute, to carry some of the weight Brant was handling. This could become the true partnership she was looking for.

"Once we remove everyone else, it's just us. And we work."

"Are you sure?" Brant asked.

She'd never been more certain of anything in all her adult life other than her love for her son. She'd had to drag herself down the aisle with Heath, but with Brant she had a feeling she'd be skipping merrily, smiling the entire time.

"I am if you are."

"It would be nice to settle things." His fingers were laced in hers. "But you know he probably won't pay you support if you marry me. And there's a chance it'll only make things worse."

She nodded. They watched each other for a long minute, the quiet reminding her of times when they were teens and would simply be in the moment, sharing it together.

"You're sure you want to do this?" Brant asked. "This isn't some wild and crazy MacFarlane trait rearing its head?"

She snorted, resenting the implication that she was still a wild and crazy kid.

"Brant…" She grew serious, squeezing his hand. "I'm more sure than when Carmichael gave me that horse I knew was gonna win rodeo."

Cookies.

Brant exhaled and gave a curt nod, his eyes dancing although he remained quiet as he turned over the engine in his truck and began driving back toward the chapel on the hill.

The lights were on, Sweetheart Creek's couple of the year still undecided.

But not for long.

APRIL STOOD in front of Old Man Lovely in her tight blue dress, feeling giddy, bold and brave. She glanced at Brant. He was smiling. They were really going to do this.

"With the power vested in me by the state of Texas, I declare you husband and wife. May your marriage be long and fruitful."

April giggled, turning to Brant.

"You may kiss the bride, if you so please." Old Man Lovely snapped a photo of them, then tipped his hat and took a step back from the polished lectern, his back curved with age.

April expected a perfunctory kiss from Brant, but he pulled her into his arms, holding her as though she'd always belonged there. Their kiss went on long enough that Old Man Lovely cleared his throat.

"Electricity's not free, you know. I already had to wait several hours for you two to find your way up the hill to my chapel. Now if you don't mind, my dogs are barking." He shifted from one "dog" to the other in his worn boots.

Brant took April by the hand and, laughing, they tore out of the tiny chapel, calling out a thank-you to Old Man Lovely, who closed the white wooden door behind them with a soft click.

"Now what?" April asked. She felt energized, like she could stay up all night.

"We celebrate?" Brant suggested.

"Yes! Should we get a drink at the Watering Hole?"

He frowned.

"Right. Let's not go back there. How about a honeymoon?" She giggled at the thought, and they both looked away from each other right after their eyes met.

They walked toward Brant's truck hand in hand.

"We can go back to my place," she suggested. "Ryan made me a bottle of sparkling wine in anticipation of my divorce. He said it should be good enough to drink by now, but I haven't had the chance to share it with anyone."

"That sounds great."

At the truck Brant held the door for April and she smiled. "Good thing I wore a dress tonight."

"Bet you didn't see your evening ending in quite this way," Brant said, and before she could climb into the truck, he tugged her closer for a kiss. His embrace felt marvelous, and she couldn't think of a better way to ring in a New Year.

A bang echoed through the quiet night, followed by a high-pitched whizzing sound. A shower of colored sparks rained down over the distant town as they turned to look.

"Fireworks," Brant murmured, his lips barely leaving hers in the process.

April wrapped her arms around his neck. "If you think those are fireworks, you just wait and see."

She laughed at his expression, then curled into his arms to watch the display from their spot beside the truck. Brant scooted away for a second to turn on the truck's radio. Each year Davis Davies, the Sweetheart Creek DJ, coordinated music to go with the fireworks show, and tonight was no exception. He'd chosen classical music, and the timing of the explosions worked well with the tune, building into crescendo after crescendo.

Brant grabbed the blanket he kept in the backseat for emergencies and wrapped it around them, drawing April into his arms. She snuggled in, content to ring in the New Year beside the man who had always been there for her. Now her husband.

She nearly giggled at the unexpected happiness that swept through her. *Husband.*

How had she not noticed Brant as something other than a friend when they were teenagers? Had her rebellious streak been so strong she'd been unable to see clearly? Or had she needed to drag herself through hell in order to find heaven?

Oh, the headaches and sleepless nights she must have caused the adults in her life. She hoped Kurt hadn't inherited her wild genetic mix. Although he likely had double, a dose from each parent.

"You used to drive Heath crazy, you know," April said, aware after she said it that Brant likely didn't want to talk about her ex on what was now their wedding night. A New Year's Eve wedding. Romantic. Special.

"What do you mean?" His body stiffened, and she wondered how his ribs felt.

"The way you stayed in touch after I got married, always checking in on me." He'd often dropped by, not only with something for her or Kurt but also to help her fix something or other in the old farmhouse.

She'd appreciated it, but it had riled Heath to know her family felt as though she needed the help, as well as checking up on.

And she had. She'd tried to be happily married to Heath, but every year she'd failed.

"He said you had a crush on me." And the fights they'd had over that. They'd been big. Some of the biggest.

"Of course I did," Brant said mildly, his arms tightening around her as he buried his face in the crook of her neck.

She laughed, unsure whether or not he was being serious. "I appreciated you checking in. For caring." Her voice broke on that last word. She forced herself to say, "I worried what your family thought of me."

"Why?"

"Because I inadvertently sent Cole away. I got pregnant. I married someone else. I know people thought I was going to marry Cole, and then I didn't."

"It wasn't you who sent Cole away. Not for that long."

"I told him I needed space to breathe, and the next thing I knew he was gone. I hadn't meant for him to leave. We'd been fighting, and I was feeling lost and confused and scared. I was afraid I was going to go back to him, even though I knew it was the wrong thing. I'd known for a long time that Cole and I were over, but I kept getting pulled back into his world and the familiarity of our ups and downs. I needed to try things with Heath. For Kurt's sake."

She waited for Brant to speak, while the fireworks rained over the town. She needed him to know the truth, more so now that their lives were entwined.

"There's more to Cole leaving," Brant said, his tone saying he didn't want to discuss it further. "Don't blame yourself."

She sighed in frustration. "You don't need to make me feel better. I know what I did to him and your family."

"April, listen." He tipped her chin his way, his gaze earnest. "If you asked for some space, and he stayed away for five years, that's not on you."

"What else would have kept him away from his family, his friends, his home?"

Brant was quiet for a long moment, his body tense.

"What?"

"I had a few words with him before he left."

"What did you say?" April turned to face him fully, ignoring the fireworks.

"I told him he should stay. That he should take care of you. That you weren't meant to be with Heath."

"Why?"

"I thought it was for the best. I was wrong."

"How do you know?"

He watched her for a long moment. "I don't. But I know that I don't want to talk about him right now."

On the radio, Davis Davies brought in the New Year, and Brant gave April a sweet kiss that curled her toes and made her forget everything but the man holding her.

"Happy New Year, April Wylder."

6

"Hello?" Out of habit, Brant had his cell phone to his ear before he was fully awake. Something was on his left arm, and his bed felt softer than the one at Carmichael's. Where had he fallen asleep?

"It's mine," April said, rolling off his arm to collect her phone from the bedside table nearest her.

"Sorry," Brant muttered groggily. He lifted his head and peered around April's bedroom. Light was streaming in through the open curtains and they were on top of the covers, fully clothed, Ryan's homemade champagne gone. April had been curled into his side, his arm tucked under her.

She sat up, gripping her phone. "Hey, Maria. Happy New Year!" Her voice sounded a bit too high, a bit too tight, as though she was hiding something.

Brant felt a jolt of panic.

They'd gotten married last night. Eloped.

It had hurt his mom to discover Ryan had done the same thing years ago. She'd found out only recently, and while she had tried to hide her pain, Brant had seen it. Now he'd repeated what

Ryan had done—slipped away to get married without telling a soul.

Why couldn't he have taken some time and treated April and his family to a proper wedding?

Because he'd been afraid she would back out?

What kind of man was he if that was his big motivator for moving fast?

He groaned and sat up, swinging his legs over the side of the bed.

"A fever?" April said into the phone. "How bad?"

"Kurt?" Brant asked, turning to watch her.

Kurt. His stepson. He was a stepdad.

He felt the smile start, but then thought of what Kurt might think or feel when he found out. The boy might not be ready to have his father replaced in his mother's heart.

Why hadn't Brant thought of that last night? He'd been so wrapped up in April's kisses and a caveman-like urge to pull her away from Heath and Cole so he could stake his claim as her number-one man. He had agreed with her argument about quieting the rumors, but hadn't thought about the ones they might start with such a hasty wedding right after her divorce, or what it could do to their families.

April's forehead crinkled, and she held her phone out to check the screen. She tapped it a few times. "It died. Can I borrow yours?" She reached across the bed, palm up. "Kurt's running a fever."

Brant's phone rang in his hand. He answered it.

"Hello?"

"You're with April," his mother stated, her voice even, revealing no hint of surprise.

They had come here last night, settled in with the champagne and a mostly ignored movie on April's tablet, sometimes kissing, sometimes laughing and joking like best friends, until they'd fallen asleep before dawn. Not once had they discussed a plan for today.

"I am. Is Kurt okay? April said he has a fever?"

"Can she come and get him? I think he'd like to be home with his mom."

"We'll be there in a few minutes." Brant ended the call before his mom could ask anything further, and stared at the black screen.

"He's okay?" April asked.

"She'd like us to pick him up."

April was already on the move. Last night she'd switched out of the tight dress, opting for a pair of sweatpants and a T-shirt. To him she looked just as sexy in the loose wear, her hair tousled and her body soft from sleep.

"Want me to make coffee?" Brant asked. He'd ditched his socks in the night, and now he walked around the bed, looking for them on the floor.

"If your mom called, I should go now."

"I can drive you."

"I've got it. You don't have to."

"I want to," he said. "Anyway, your car's still at the Watering Hole."

April's eyes met his for a moment, and they stared at each other across the bed. Brant could see the doubts, the worries in his wife's eyes. All their arguments about why they should elope seemed less convincing in the light of day.

"We can discuss things later," Brant said. "We should get Kurt, but maybe stop at the diner and grab a quick coffee to go. I have a feeling we might not get a break for at least an hour or two, and the extra minute it takes to zip in will be worth it."

April nodded and headed for the bedroom door.

"Hey," he said, snagging her hand and pulling her to a halt. He watched her for a second before gently tipping her chin upward for a good-morning kiss and a reminder of all the reasons they'd said "I do."

APRIL FOLLOWED BRANT, her husband, out of her home, then locked the door behind them. She'd agreed to his plan to pop into the diner for a quick coffee and breakfast sandwich to go, as she didn't want to count on him helping out with Kurt so she could refuel herself. It was one thing for him to marry her in Mr. Lovely's chapel at midnight, and quite another to expect him to tend to her sick son bright and early the next morning.

As they drove the few short blocks to the Longhorn Diner, the logistics of having a husband ran through April's mind. Was Brant going to move in with her and Kurt? So far her son had been adjusting well to living apart from Heath, who had often been out on the road, working, before their separation. But she knew her ex's broken promises impacted him. Having Brant step in as a more permanent father figure so quickly might make things worse for Kurt and Heath's relationship. And Kurt might even reject Brant—even though he'd been referring to him as Daddy Brant.

Last night, marriage had felt like such a straightforward solution, but this morning it felt full of expectations and traditions their relationship wasn't ready for.

"Maybe we can wait to tell Kurt once he's feeling better," she suggested.

"There are a few things we didn't think through, aren't there?" Brant said mildly as he maneuvered his truck into a parking spot in front of the diner.

April couldn't help but laugh. It was so ridiculous. In some ways she hadn't changed. She'd jumped in with both feet, and even though the whole arrangement was fraught with difficulties, it still felt nothing but right.

"If I'm going to elope with anyone, I'm glad it was you," she said, opening her door and sliding off the seat, her boots hitting the asphalt.

"Hey."

April turned to Brant. He was still in the driver's seat, his arm draped over the steering wheel. "Is all of this a secret until we figure out a game plan?"

She hesitated a second, quickly considering their options, then gave a quick nod. "Probably for the best."

"Okay." He removed his keys and climbed out, holding the door open for her once they reached the diner. The Christmas decorations were still up, and as per Sweetheart Creek tradition, the place was packed.

April began beelining it to the back, hoping Mrs. Fisher already had breakfast sandwiches ready to go, as she often did the morning of New Year's Day.

Brant took a large step to catch up with her, putting them shoulder to shoulder as they walked the aisle between the booths to their right and the checkered-cloth-covered tables to their left. People began applauding and smiling.

April turned to look behind them, then at Brant. He shared her confusion with a shrug. Someone clinked a fork against a water glass, and the room quickly echoed with the sound.

April's heart nearly stopped. It was the glass-clinking from weddings, when the guests wanted the newlyweds to kiss.

"What's going on?" April asked, her voice strangled.

"The good news is out!" Mrs. Fisher said merrily, embracing her in a hug that smelled of bacon and hairspray.

"What?" April shot Brant a look of alarm and his face paled.

"You're Mr. Lovely's couple of the year!" Mrs. Fisher clasped her hands in front of her dazzling pink Western blouse. "I just knew it would be you two. You're in the paper's online edition already. We were wondering when you'd surface." She winked and nudged April. "A little earlier than I'd predicted."

April had forgotten about the paper. Old Man Lovely would have sent their names and photo in first thing this morning, or even last night. The news would be all over town already, as the online edition was one of the first things most people—including herself—checked on New Year's Day. She'd been tickled when the paper went online, as it meant she could get the Couple of the Year news without having to get out of her bathrobe. At the moment, though, she wasn't quite so pleased with the speed of progress in Sweetheart Creek.

"I'm sorry we can't stop and talk about it. We're in a bit of a hurry," Brant said, guiding Mrs. Fisher toward the back counter. He smiled and nodded to people as they moved through the room.

"Are you now?" Mrs. Fisher teased.

"Elopements are bad, bad news," grumbled Uncle Henry from his spot at the counter. His white hair was sticking up at the back as if he'd forgotten to brush it that morning. "You'd think you would've learned from Ryan's mistake."

"Henry," Garfield Goodwin said in a hushed voice, his gaze darting to Brant and April, "April's in the family way." Eyeing her midriff with a kind smile, he asked, "Aren't you, dear?"

"No." April couldn't stop shaking her head. "I'm not. We didn't. I didn't. We're not. No." She took a breath, hoping to form a rational reply that sounded less guilty.

"It's all right now." Garfield reached out and patted her hand. "We all saw you two whispering around town whenever Heath was away last fall."

"Brant was helping me get situated so I could leave my marriage."

"We know, dear." Garfield's smile was kind, his unwillingness to bend his thinking as strong as the steel beams holding up the town's several-ton water tower.

April cringed. By eloping, they'd inadvertently reinforced

everyone's worst assumptions about her and Brant. How had she not considered that possibility last night?

She looked to Brant for help, but his mouth was tucked into a tight frown and his hands were flexing open and closed. He cleared his throat and leaned over the counter, his attention directed at Mrs. Fisher, who was clearly enjoying the gossip. "My mom called. Kurt has a fever, and we're heading over to pick him up, but we need two coffees to go."

"And a breakfast sandwich," April added. She glanced at Brant. "Make it two, please."

Mrs. Fisher's expression turned sympathetic. "I hope he's okay. Poor boy. Didn't he have a fever last month, too?" She poured two cups of coffee and put on plastic lids.

"A spoonful of cod liver oil will do him up right," Garfield advised.

"Boys don't play in the dirt enough these days," Uncle Henry added.

Mrs. Fisher put the cups in a tray and slid it across the counter. "On the house. For our town's couple of the year." With a wink, she passed two wrapped sandwiches that had been waiting under the heating lamp April's way.

April scooped up the food while Brant took the tray. They turned, April's focus on the door. Everyone in the diner seemed to be smiling at them, while whispers swirled across the tables.

The clinking started up again.

"We'd better go with this," Brant muttered. He turned, putting the coffees back on the counter. He flashed the room a bright smile, then wrapped an arm around April's waist, bending her to him as he landed his hot lips on hers.

Her body relaxed, and she gripped his coat collar for support, the breakfast sandwiches long forgotten. Everyone in the diner whooped and cheered as Brant released her. He held their linked hands in the air, grabbed the coffees and pulled her toward the door.

"THERE GOES OUR SECRET," Brant said as they climbed into his truck. "I forgot how fast Old Man Lovely is with getting the news out."

"He is fast," April agreed, thumbing open the lid of her coffee cup. She was staring out the windshield, her expression blank, the breakfast sandwiches sitting untouched on the seat between them. They looked deformed, as if she'd squeezed them at some point.

Brant glanced at his wife again, seeking clues. "Do you still want to keep it quiet with Kurt for a bit?" he asked gently.

She nodded.

A few minutes later Brant turned down the Sweet Meadows Ranch driveway, his scalding coffee already half consumed due to his on-call-veterinarian habit of trying to get it in him while it was still hot.

He tried to convince himself he regretted last night's spontaneous actions, but couldn't manage to. His only regrets were the difficulties their quick marriage were likely to give April.

Brant parked in front of the ranch house, and they both got out and headed up the steps, knowing Maria would have opted to settle Kurt there while she cooked breakfast for the family.

The door opened before Brant could turn the knob.

His mom stood in the doorway, her hands on her hips.

"What do you two think you're up to?" She glanced over her shoulder, no doubt on the lookout for Kurt. She stepped onto the porch, carefully closing the door behind her. "Old Man Lovely?"

The hurt in her expression was clear, and Brant felt a flush of shame. "We were trying to stop the rumors." He winced at the feeble excuse.

"More like trying to start some."

"It's not Brant's fault," April blurted.

"Yes, it is." He turned to her. There was no way she was shouldering the blame.

"No, it's not."

"I wanted to marry you, and I did," he said firmly.

April's cheeks sucked in as she inhaled, and she gave him the most grateful look he'd ever seen.

Brant turned his attention back to Maria. "I'm sorry, Mom. I know you would have preferred something more traditional."

Her hands were still on her hips, the chilly January morning not seeming to affect her despite her lack of a sweater. "First, I hear you boys are fighting with Heath at the Watering Hole. Then this? This is not how I raised you, Brant Boaz Wylder."

April's voice was remorseful as she spoke. "It was my fault, Mrs. Wylder. I have a history of making bad judgment calls."

Brant felt the words hit him hard in the chest, and he dropped his eyes after catching his mom's pointed glance. Maria sighed heavily, rocked back on her heels, then shook her head as she drew them into the house. "You two had better come in and figure out how you're going to tell Kurt you got married last night."

"You got married!" Kurt exclaimed in delight. His face was pale, and he was a bit wobbly as he came running to Brant, before throwing himself into his arms.

"What are you doing up?" Maria scolded.

As Brant caught the boy, his worries dropped off him like water off a duck. He gave Kurt a big hug, then stood up with him in his arms. A tear trickled down April's cheek, and she and Brant shared a watery smile over Kurt's shoulder.

This moment—this feeling among the three of them—was worth it all.

"We did, but…" Brant glanced at April, letting her know she should take the lead on how to frame their spontaneous decision.

Kurt's arms wound tight around Brant's neck. "I made a wish last night on a shooting star. Gramps Carmichael told me not to tell anyone because it might not come true. But it did. And now I can tell everyone that you're my daddy."

Brant's heart swelled, and he didn't dare look at either woman to catch their expressions. He wanted to preserve this sweet moment just the way it was. No doubts or unspoken worries. Just a boy's happiness, love and overwhelming acceptance.

"Well then," Maria said, after clearing her throat. "You had best get this boy home and to bed. Although good luck keeping him there."

She couldn't seem to hide her growing smile, and the tension in Brant's chest eased.

As Maria filled April in on the details of Kurt's fever, Brant held him in his arms. The child was warm, and he wrapped him in a blanket from the living room so he wouldn't get a chill while they walked from the house to the truck. As he tucked him closer, Brant smiled. He was happy. He was married. Therefore, he must be a happily married man.

Cole shuffled into the room, sleepy-eyed. "What's up?" His gaze moving first to April, then to Brant and Kurt. "I thought you guys weren't coming until noon to share the joy of Mom taking us each by the ear and scolding us for last night's fight."

"Thanks, by the way," Brant said quietly, letting his brother know he appreciated the interference he'd provided, so he and April could escape from the scene.

Cole held eye contact and nodded wordlessly.

"Kurt has a fever." April picked up her son's overnight bag and headed for the door.

"Brant's my new daddy," Kurt said happily, still snuggled in his arms. Brant felt his chest expand and a protective strength grow within him.

"That's nice," Cole said mildly. "Hope you feel better soon, little buddy."

"No, Uncle Cole. Brant's my *daddy*," Kurt said, insisting impatiently when Cole didn't acknowledge the change in status. "I made a wish with Gramps, and they got *married*."

Cole's eyes widened, and he shed the grogginess of sleep as he pivoted to stare at Brant and April. "Old Man Lovely?" His tone held both awe and disbelief.

Brant gave a small nod. Cole continued to gape for a moment, and then his mouth twitched as though he was fighting a smile. "You moving out?" he asked, controlling his grin. "'Cause I kind of like your room, and I feel guilty taking it from you. I know you don't care for Carmichael's crappy spare bed."

"We'll keep you in the loop," Brant said, nodding to April, who opened the door. "Happy New Year."

As Brant shut the door behind them, he heard Cole say to their mom, "Let's hope their elopement turns out better than Ryan's did."

***

AFTER BRANT SETTLED Kurt on the couch in front of the television in the living room, April tucked a blanket around him and poured him some ginger ale, surprised at how insistent Kurt was that Brant tend to him. She sipped the last of her diner coffee in the kitchen doorway and watched as Brant cared for her son.

"I'll watch cartoons now, Daddy Brant." Kurt waved him away, and with conflicting emotions April let the new name sink in. When he looked up at her from his spot by the couch, his eyes were as blue as she'd ever seen them. He was in his stocking feet, no boots, no hat. Having him knelt beside her son, still rumpled from sleeping in his clothes, handsome and unshaven, she was struck by how intimate and domestic the moment felt, as if Brant belonged here, in her home—his home.

He slowly rose to his feet and walked over to where she stood in the kitchen doorway.

"He's happy," April said, swallowing a lump of emotion as she gestured to Kurt.

"He is," Brant agreed.

Tension built between them from words unspoken, and she headed for the coffeemaker, dropping her empty takeout cup in the trash on the way by. The breakfast sandwich was long gone, and after such a short sleep last night, she needed more caffeine to help her sort through everything running through her mind and heart.

Kurt was happy. Brant seemed to be, too, despite his attempts to appear casual. If she gave herself long enough to think about it, she'd admit she was happy, as well.

She was scared, though. Marriage meant a lot more than liking each other and kissing with passion. They hadn't even been on an official date, or said they loved one another.

Kurt, however, was all over the idea. Would she be putting Brant's name down in one of the parent boxes when she registered her son for school next fall? Or was last night's spontaneous move going to wind up breaking Kurt's heart and creating attachment issues?

"So?" April leaned her hip against the counter. She crossed her arms. "How are we going to manage this? It's not a secret any longer. Everyone knows, except maybe Wade Ross, and that's only because he's probably still passed out in a ditch on his tractor unless Myles rescued him." She paused for a breath. "What are you looking for in our relationship?"

Brant considered her question, his attention on his thumbnail.

"Well?" April snapped. "Say something."

"I don't regret getting married." He met her eyes, his own steady and calm. "Do you?"

She inhaled with a hiss. The rumors they'd faced in the diner seemed to buffet her like a strong wind. She couldn't think about how she felt right now. Everything was so fresh and uncertain, and she feared doing damage to Kurt or Brant with last night's spur-of-the-moment decision.

"I don't regret it, but we sure didn't improve the things being said about us." She turned, wiped the counter around the coffeemaker, then retrieved two ceramic mugs from the cupboard above and set them out.

Brant slid his hands around her waist with a sureness that grounded her. After a moment, she allowed herself to relax against him, curious to see what it might feel like to have someone try to calm her storm instead of build off it.

"I don't care what everyone says," he stated.

She turned in his arms so she could see his face. "You heal and fix and rescue, and do all these wonderful, amazing, caring things. And I just blasted into your life and made you look like a home-wrecker." She bit her lips to hold in the emotion.

"And was I?" He stroked her cheek with a thumb, that amused twinkle dancing in his eyes even though she growled in frustration.

"No. Maybe. I don't know anymore." She shifted out of his embrace and started wiping the counter again. She hadn't expected a relationship with Brant when she'd been ending her marriage, but in a secret back corner of her mind she'd been hoping. Hoping for kisses. Hoping he might rescue her heart. Hoping she could win his. Hoping he would notice her as a woman worth pursuing, and that she could find something stable and amazing with him like she saw her friends having.

And now she had the potential to do so, and she feared messing it up. How did you go from a spur-of-the-moment marriage to making things work in a forever-and-ever sense?

Even when she'd been dating Cole all those years ago, she'd had fleeting thoughts about the smooth relationships Brant seemed to have. She'd wondered what it would be like to be kissed by a man who took the time to pause and really look at a woman. She'd catch herself and scoff, telling herself she was fantasizing about something that would certainly be boring.

But it wasn't. Not by a long shot.

She knew this was what she wanted, but she wasn't sure how to make it happen.

Realizing she'd been lost in her own thoughts, she glanced at Brant. His head was tipped to the side, a dented ring in his hair showing where his hat had been sitting. He was watching her.

Her jaw loosened as their eyes met, and the breath rushed from her lungs.

How long had she been in love with Brant?

Forever? A day?

Was everyone right? Had she really left Heath because of him?

She placed her palms against her cheeks and began laughing as an unfamiliar sensation flowed through her. It almost felt as though she was filling up with helium.

She loved Brant. And she had married him.

How had that even happened?

Why was she stressed and worried? Her dream had come true!

She laughed harder as she dropped the cloth and stepped forward, feeling light. Her hands glided over his shoulders to meet at the nape of his neck. There was something about Brant that had always settled her inner whirlwind, and even in this morning's chaos, it was no different.

Was that what love was?

Their relationship had serious potential, and there was nothing to hold her back. Nothing at all. And while they might not be fully ready for marriage, she vowed she was going to do everything she could to reach for it, claim it, savor it and protect it. This was what she had been hoping and wishing for.

"Why did it take me so long to see this?" she asked.

"And what is 'this'?" Brant asked, then gave her a kiss.

"What we have."

"It's something good, isn't it?" His next, longer kiss made her toes curl.

"You see it, too?"

"I do."

"Brant?"

"Hmm?"

"No regrets?"

"Absolutely none."

That was all she needed to hear.

BRANT SMILED against April's lips. No regrets.

He tightened his arms around her, lifting her into the air and spinning her around in the middle of the kitchen. She giggled and he kissed her again.

"Mom?" Kurt called from the living room.

April frowned and braced Brant's face with her hands. "Duty calls," she whispered, kissing him again. She let out a purr of contentment when it lingered into something with heat.

"*Mom?*"

April sighed against Brant's mouth. "Just a minute," she called. She tapped Brant's lips. "Hold that thought." She slipped from his arms and headed to the living room.

Brant looked around the kitchen, wondering what their next step was. Should he move in? Somehow that felt premature, but not moving in would make their marriage seem fake.

His phone rang, and he lifted the device to his ear. It was Levi.

"What's up?" Brant asked.

"We've got a stuck calf. I can't get it to turn. Any chance you could pop by?"

They had a winter birthing plan in place as one of Levi's ideas for the ranch, but this cow was literally ahead of the herd, having slipped through the fence and met up with a bull earlier in the year.

"Sure. Be there in a few minutes."

"Wait, shouldn't you be on your honeymoon?" Levi teased.

Brant opened his mouth, his gaze darting to the doorway where April had exited. Were they going to have a honeymoon? An official wedding night? A reception? It wouldn't be long before the townsfolk started sending over gifts as part of the Couple of the Year tradition. And they'd plan a reception, too, if memory served.

Brant smiled. He wouldn't mind any of that.

"Yeah, probably," he said cheerily. He raised his voice. "But no honeymoon today. Right, April?"

"Honeymoon?" she asked with a touch of incredulity.

"Wouldn't that be fun?"

His words were met with silence, and he peeked around the corner into the living room. April was holding a wet facecloth in her hands, looking a bit stunned. "Um…"

"Let's aim for February," he suggested.

"Very romantic," Levi stated with a dry tone.

"I thought so," he said agreeably, ignoring his brother's tone.

"So you're finally going to get her a dog?"

Brant turned back into the kitchen, and poured himself a cup of coffee even though the pot hadn't finished brewing. "What's this?"

"April. Dog."

"Why? I have a dog." Dodge spent a lot of time at the ranch or out on vet calls with him, but eventually he'd likely start living here if he didn't mind being in town.

There was a pause on the other end of the line. April had mentioned wanting a dog. Had she enlisted Levi's help? The silence continued, and Brant said, "Tell me."

"It's just a thing Laura noticed."

"What thing?"

"Well, you found a rescue for Laura, Karen, Carly, Mom, and even Daisy-Mae and Jackie."

"So? They all wanted a dog. Just like you and Myles and Ryan. Even Carmichael."

"Yeah."

His brother was closing up. Brant could hear it in his voice. He was going to turn to business any second, and the opportunity to figure out what was going on would be missed.

"So what does it have to do with a certain someone else?" He lowered his voice and peeked into the living room again. April was bent over Kurt, smoothing his hair back from his forehead and talking to him in a soothing tone.

Levi sighed, no doubt wishing he hadn't brought up the topic. Discussing this sort of stuff wasn't anywhere near his comfort zone.

"What?" Brant insisted.

He could hear Laura in the background, demanding to join the conversation. Moments later Levi said sullenly, "Putting you on speaker. Here's Laura."

"What Levi's trying to say is this: Get April a dog. She's going to have doubts about whether you approve of her."

"Uh, I married her," Brant said, with a chuckle of amusement. That was basically the stamp of approval, wasn't it? "And what does a dog have to do with how I feel about her?"

Laura sighed, and Brant could imagine her rolling her eyes at Levi.

"Just spit it out, Laura." He'd known her only a few months, but the woman had a kind heart and he knew he could take whatever she delivered, whether he wanted to hear it or not.

When she still didn't speak, he said, "April knows how I feel."

"What women know and what we feel are two different things," she said patiently. "You may have married her, but you haven't shown her she's passed the test."

"There's a test?" He caught himself. He was uncomfortable

with this conversation, and instead of listening, he was being sarcastic. But why? He cared for April. He simply hadn't found her the right dog yet, due to timing in her life. Right?

"In case you haven't noticed, when you approve of a woman as part of your inner circle you give her a dog." Laura paused meaningfully.

He nodded as he thought that through. "Yeah, okay." Although that made him sound as though he was pawning off strays on people who might not want a pet, just because he liked them and felt they should have a pet.

"You haven't given her a dog. And she's asked. Even Kurt has asked."

"She's got a lot going on right now. The last thing she needs is something else pulling at her attention and draining her finances." Brant glanced through the doorway yet again, noting the paleness of April's face, the smudges under her eyes. It wasn't the right time for a pet, even though the right beast might make a relaxing companion.

It definitely wasn't the right moment. She hadn't even retrieved her beloved horse, Cookies, from Heath's yet. Another animal would surely be too much to take on right now.

"Afraid it'll one-up you when it comes to attention?" Laura asked, a wicked note in her tone.

Levi laughed and Brant scowled, saying, "Not funny."

"She's kidding. April's always had a wilder, adventure-seeking side," his brother said, "but marriage? Maybe a few years ago we would have found her at Old Man Lovely's, but these days...?"

"What are you saying?" Brant asked sharply.

"She didn't marry you on a whim."

"I know that. And I'm sure the right dog will come along."

"You could find her one within a week if you wanted to," Levi added. "So..." He paused as though looking at his girlfriend, before asking, "What are you afraid of?"

"I'm not afraid," Brant grumbled, ignoring the itchy feeling that was suddenly prickling him.

If he truly had fears, he was sure it had nothing to do with getting April a dog.

But if that was true, why hadn't he found her a furry companion? Not because of finances, because he could cover that, if need be. So why?

He ended the call, unable to shake a phantom sensation of an upcoming rejection. He grabbed his coat off the hook in the small entry, saying to April and Kurt, "We've got a stuck calf at the ranch. Seems insistent on coming out the wrong way."

April winced.

"I'll be back in an hour or two."

She nodded, stood and took a step toward him, then stopped as if uncertain.

Brant strode to her, wrapped an arm around her waist and gave her a long kiss. This was one thing he wasn't afraid of. And this was how he planned to say goodbye to his wife every day.

He released her, and she stumbled as though the kiss had weakened her knees. Her cheeks flushed.

"I can bring lunch from the diner if you're hungry and haven't wasted away by then."

April laughed. "Are you kidding? Your mom won't let you leave empty-handed."

Brant chuckled as he pulled on his boots. That was quite likely, especially since they had a sick kid at home.

Home. Family. Kid. Wife.

He inhaled, savoring the sensation of having it all, then gave April another quick kiss, murmuring, "Welcome to the family."

"I was already part of the family. And as for calling me April Wylder, I haven't decided about that yet."

"Fair enough. I'll always think of you as a bratty MacFarlane, anyway." He chuckled and sidestepped her playful attack, then, realizing it was a good excuse to get physical, stepped into her arms. He let her wrestle with him, ignoring the twinge in his ribs from where Heath had landed a blow last night, and finally stole another kiss before zipping out the door.

Grinning, he hustled down the walk to his truck, thinking this whole marriage thing was something he could definitely get used to. And that, truly, there wasn't a single thing to be afraid of when it came to him and April.

7

*B*rant met up with April in the back of his clinic, sharing a coffee before their workday started. Kurt's fever had broken later on New Year's Day, and he'd had the weekend to recuperate, as well as April's Monday off, before returning to day care today.

Brant hadn't moved in yet, and they needed to figure out what they were going to do. And not just because his clinic had been flooded with well-wishers yesterday, and people asking if he needed help moving into April's.

Sharing a house might be too much too soon, and he worried that if they didn't build a base for their relationship they could easily end up slipping into a freak-out zone. Above all else, he wanted this marriage to last.

"I was thinking," he began.

"Uh-oh," April teased.

"What did they call dating in the old days? Courting? We should do that."

"We should court each other?"

"Well, we could call it dating."

"We're *married*, Brant."

Her tone made his idea seem silly. "I know, but I don't expect you to want me to move in right away, or jump in with Kurt like I'm his dad. You have your life and ways of doing things, and I need to respect that."

She was listening now, her blue eyes fixed on him.

"We can ease into things."

"Ease into things," she said, her expression becoming wary. It was as though she was running through a list of doubts. "And you don't want to live with me?"

"That's not it at all. I want this to work out, April." He scooted his chair closer to hers, nudging her cowboy boot with his own. "And I was thinking we'd start by dating. Not that friend stuff we used to do, but proper dates. Get to know each other on a different level."

He could focus on her, show her she was the center of his attention. No distractions. Just the two of them.

"You already asked me out for this Friday. I said yes," April stated.

"I know. But I'm talking about an actual plan. Like date night every Friday for a month, and me moving in on the weekend. We can assess things as we go, and take it from there."

"So romantic."

He sighed. "So we just jump in and fight over stupid stuff like socks left on the couch and who's supposed to put Kurt to bed and how much sugar he's allowed to have?"

"Fine. We'll go out Friday and Saturday, and you move in this weekend."

"Friday *and* Saturday? Don't you want to spend that time with Kurt?"

"Heath has him every other week."

"Right." Brant didn't mention that the man had yet to do more than take Kurt for the odd day here and there.

"You have better plans for your Saturdays?" April leaned

forward, her wheeled chair gliding sideways. The challenge in her voice was clear.

"No." Brant straightened.

"Good, because you'll be all mine."

He liked the sound of that.

There were still potential flaws in their plan, though.

"What if we can't find a babysitter—on your weeks—or I get called in for an emergency?"

"Looking for excuses, Wylder?" She locked her feet around his and wheeled her chair closer until their legs touched.

"No."

"Glad to hear it." There was determination in her tone as well as a hint of triumph, as though she'd just scored something.

He wasn't sure what, but was certain it meant something good.

A FEW HOURS later April let out a sigh of relief, as Jackie pivoted to leave the veterinary clinic. Her matchmaking friend had a lot of advice on what she and Brant should do now that they were married. Jackie also kept saying how perfect she thought they were together.

Expectations for this marriage were upping the ante faster than the gossip had spread around town. Brant's slow and steady plan was looking like something to cling to in what was quickly becoming a bit of a whirlwind.

They'd mostly hidden out with Kurt over the weekend, not acting married so much as settling into the idea. But it had been nice. Really nice. One of her favorite weekends in recent memory, for sure. The sweet, stolen kisses hadn't been too bad, either.

"Hey, Jackie, April, " Daisy-Mae called, entering the reception area. She sashayed over to the counter, wearing a sweater so tight

April could practically identify her bra's brand. The woman looked good. How was she still single? "Just dropping this off." She set a small wrapped box on the counter.

"What's this?" April asked, lifting it.

"A wedding present."

"Oh." She stared at it for a second. "Thank you."

"Mine's coming on Wednesday," Jackie said quickly. "I had to order it in."

"That's fine. Really. You guys didn't need to."

Jackie looked offended. "Of course we did. You two finally tied the knot."

"To give Heath a message he can't ignore," Daisy-Mae added with a satisfied smile. "Brant's a good man."

"I didn't get married to spite Heath."

Daisy-Mae propped an elbow on the counter. "Brant's such a great guy. There's no hardship pretending to be married to him!" She let out a light laugh and April felt a surge of possessiveness that had her clenching her jaw and pushing her shoulders back.

"What?" Jackie frowned. "They're actually married."

"He offered to act like he was engaged to me once, when that guy from Riverbend wouldn't take a hint." Daisy-Mae's tone lost its dreamy quality for a beat, but then her smile returned. "Brant's the last decent man." She pivoted, gliding out the door in a way that hinted at her beauty pageant past.

Jackie raised her eyebrows at April. "Have fun with that rumor."

There was a new one every hour, it felt like. At least they didn't seem to freak out Brant, and luckily, so far his calmness was proving to be contagious. At this point, people were going to talk no matter what they did. And the truth was, she was doing what she wanted.

Once Jackie left, April locked the clinic door, flipping over the sign that said Closed for Lunch.

"Hungry?" Brant asked, appearing from the back. He was in

jeans and an insulated navy vest with the clinic's logo on the breast pocket. He looked so handsome, and she felt a jolt of pleasure remembering he was hers. All hers. Violet Granger, who'd given him flirtatious looks at New Year's, could go find someone else. And even Daisy-Mae who'd been gushing over him could keep on looking for her own Mr. Right, because Brant Wylder, the sweetest man in Sweetheart Creek, was officially taken.

"I brought a lunch," April said, moving past him on her way to the staff fridge in the back. He caught her in his arms, giving her a kiss.

"I was thinking the diner," he murmured, nuzzling her neck and sending shivers down her back. "My treat."

April wrinkled her nose and slid from his arms. Facing half the town in the diner wasn't an appetizing idea. Too many rumors. Too much speculation. She was pretty sure nearly everyone had heard the news of their marriage by now—including Heath, although so far he hadn't made a peep. It had been five days now, and as far as she knew, he was on the road again, leaving Kurt hanging.

She still needed to get her rodeo horse from the farm, but she had no plan to go over there anytime soon—even if Heath was away. Especially if what she and Brant had done had truly left Heath feeling spiteful, as Daisy-Mae had assumed. April didn't want to see that side of Heath right now.

"We can't hide out forever," Brant warned.

"Yes, we can."

He let out a huff of amusement. "Good luck with that."

She headed to the fridge and pulled out her container of leftover casserole from last night. She'd offered Brant some for his lunch, but he said he'd bring something from the ranch, which was where he was still staying.

"Daisy-Mae left us a gift," she stated.

Brant smiled. "That's nice of her. What is it?"

"I haven't opened it yet."

"Waiting for me?" He tugged her away from the fridge, which sported Kurt's Christmas painting, and wrapped his arms around her. "There were a lot of well-wishers in here all day yesterday, you know."

"They're confused over why you haven't moved in yet." Even Kurt was asking.

"I've had a lot of offers to help me move my stuff." He was smiling, not at all fazed. "Don't worry, April. We've set a date—I move in this weekend."

"Our elopement looks impulsive."

"It was."

She couldn't help but smile. "I know, but…"

"Come on," he coaxed, dropping his arms and gently grasping her hand. "The longer we put off facing the town again, the worse it's going to feel when we finally do."

April sighed. "Fine."

They headed out the clinic's back door to take a shortcut to Main Street and the Longhorn Diner. The January sunshine was bright, and they squinted after the building's artificial light.

It was Tuesday, which meant the special was chicken potpie, one of Brant's favorites. The thought put some pep in his step.

"Watch out, Bill's on a rampage," he cautioned, steering April onto the street half a block from the restaurant.

April looked over her shoulder, spotting Sweetheart Creek's well-known armadillo, an ornery old coot of a mammal, ambling down the sidewalk. He was making awful sounds at anyone who dared cross his path today.

"I'm surprised someone hasn't requested you relocate him," April said, referring to Brant's secondary job as one of the county's animal control officers. Bill had a reputation for being a nuisance, and there had been mention of having him moved to some woods away from town.

"He has a drink named after him at the Watering Hole." Brant gestured toward the weather-worn saloon on the opposite side of the road, as if that explained everything. "He's practically our town mascot. There's even talk of painting his picture on the Welcome sign."

"You're serious?"

"Word on the street is that he'll be on it." The town council had voted to refresh the town's Welcome signs and include the fact that Sweetheart Creek was now home to a football state championship title.

"Well, then you definitely can't relocate him."

"Agreed."

Brant placed a hand at April's lower back to hurry her along as a truck rolled down the street. She hoped he found a reason to keep it there, finding his body heat warm and welcoming as it spread through her.

The driver, Travis Nestner, the town mayor, leaned out his window to say, "Happy New Year, y'all! And congratulations!"

"Back at you!" Brant called, as they both waved to him. "People are asking if we're going to take a honeymoon," he added in a low voice.

"They're asking me if we have a gift registry."

"So? Are we?"

"A honeymoon sounds expensive."

"We could put it on our gift registry."

April laughed before realizing he was serious.

"We rushed this so much," she mused. "I don't know what's proper." Nothing about their marriage felt real, and the idea of setting up a registry or planning a honeymoon felt strange.

"We may have rushed into things," Brant admitted, his tone more serious, and April tensed. This was where he realized he was just helping out a friend, and broke up with her, wasn't it? This was where everything turned into a colossal mess. He would leave her, and she would look like an impulsive fool who had subjected her son to unnecessary emotional trauma. Meanwhile, Brant would have a tarnished image of being played for a fool while trying to rescue another woman who didn't want him. Even though he'd be the one cutting the cord this time, and she very much *did* want him.

"But as I said before, our marriage may have been spontaneous, but it's not something I regret." He stopped, waiting for her to face him.

Her chest flooded with relief.

"So what do we do?" she murmured.

"Stop thinking." The tension in Brant's features softened. He gently brushed her cheek with his thumb in a move so tender she relaxed. When she was with Brant, nothing else mattered.

"You're going to have to kiss me to make that happen."

"That can be arranged."

"Well? Don't keep me waiting, Wylder."

"Agree to a honeymoon first."

She almost laughed, her nervousness taking hold again. But looking into Brant's steady, calm gaze, she knew she needed to let go of her fears and continue to follow his lead if she wanted any chance of making this elopement work like a real marriage.

With all the trimmings.

BRANT WAITED at the back counter of the diner for their lunch order. April had been waylaid by a tableful of women, and he'd promised to put in their order with Mrs. Fisher, when they'd started talking about registries and such.

"Weren't you just driving out of town?" Brant asked Travis Nestner as the mayor took the stool beside him.

"Yup. But thought I'd pop by and ask if you've put any more thought into joining that study on breeding schedules being run by the HCCC."

The Hill Country Community College animal husbandry study. Right.

"April?" Brant called. "Can you help me out a minute?" Maybe he could use one of those coupons she'd given him at Christmas to escape this conversation. He hated to say no, but where was he going to find the time to do this—especially now that he had a marriage to build?

Daisy-Mae, who was sipping a coffee farther down the counter, drawled, "Honey, a woman needs longer than a minute. I dated a single dad once and know how it goes." She muttered to herself, "Not doing that again." Her voice became louder as she asked, "When are y'all going to take that honeymoon?"

April turned pink as she came to join them.

"I'd offer to take Kurt," Daisy-Mae added, "but I know nothing about kids."

"We haven't planned anything yet," April said, "but I'm sure when we do either Maria or Heath will take him."

Daisy-Mae choked at hearing Heath's name, but covered it quickly. "Let me know if y'all need anything."

"He's welcome to stay with us. We already have a zoo," Travis said, referring to their triplets. "Another munchkin underfoot won't drive us around the bend."

"I couldn't do that to you and Donna," April said, nestling into Brant's side as though she'd always belonged there. Without a second thought, he planted a kiss on the top of her head. She glanced up, her face open and happy. He could spend his entire afternoon here.

"Honestly, the distraction would be welcome. The girls are getting competitive about who gets the most attention from Donna and me."

Brant edged April closer, warmed by the idea of a honeymoon and wishing the diner was the kind of place he could sweep her into a soulful kiss without causing a scene. "We should plan a getaway."

April laughed nervously.

"It would be good for us."

She met his gaze, and he could see her thinking that over.

"Before you get distracted," Travis said to April, "can you convince this guy to join our study?"

"You think I have sway?" April pressed her hand against her chest and her eyebrows lifted. She had a lot more pull than Brant wanted to admit, and he had a feeling if these two ganged up on him he'd be joining the study that very afternoon.

"Levi's already in, and it would be nice to have a veterinarian with some ranching experience on the panel. Levi said this study is an extension of what you're already doing. Except, of course, you'd have some researchers, science and grants backing you." Seeing that Brant still wasn't convinced, Travis added, "It would be a meaningful way to contribute to local animal health."

"I don't have time," Brant said, frowning. It was a long-term study, and the number of herds he'd have to check on wouldn't be insignificant. "Sorry, Travis."

"You have fewer chores on the ranch now that Cole's back," April said. And Levi hired Owen Lancaster to come help out since he and his dad had that falling out on their own ranch."

Brant flashed her a dark look as thanks for her unwanted helpfulness. It was true Cole was working on fitting himself into the ranch duties once again, taking over chores and freeing up time for his brothers over the past two weeks. But would he stay long enough that Brant could rely on that newly freed-up time?

"I'm still running a clinic, as well as acting as the county's animal control officer. Plus—" he snugged his arm around April's shoulders, bringing her tight against him "—I'm a newlywed. I have marital duties." He placed a kiss against April's temple and enjoyed how her expression softened.

"Sounds like you might have excess energy and time to burn, seeing as you two aren't living together yet." Travis winked.

"I'm moving in on the weekend," Brant said.

"The study will help more cattle than you can through the

clinic," April pointed out, and Brant frowned at her. "Don't veterinarians sign an oath about helping animals?"

Brant chuckled at her argument. "Are you trying to get rid of me?"

"Wouldn't you want other ranchers using a system that's better for their herds?"

Brant gave a shake of his head and looked to the heavens as though summoning help. "I'm only one man."

"Come on, you know you want to," Travis said. "The data and analysis will be specific to our region. It'll be good for the town."

"Trying to get reelected?"

April patted Brant's chest. "My husband is all about what's best for the herds. Whatever's easiest on the calves and mothers, right, hon?" That was the first time she'd used a term of endearment, and he liked it. "I'm sure he truly doesn't have the time to do that, or he'd say yes to saving more calves from summer birthing issues like dehydration, as well as preventing unnecessary difficult births."

Brant's unease grew, and he sighed at the way April was playing to his weakness. He dropped his arm, releasing her as she bent to pick up a fork that had fallen to the floor.

The beadwork on the back pockets on her jeans sparkled under the lights and her curves kept his attention until she straightened again. Oh, those curves.

"I'll help Brant with the paperwork," she said, rejoining them. "So you can scratch that argument."

She was trying to get him to do something good to help any reputation damage she thought she might have caused, wasn't she? She snuggled up to him again and the last of his resistance started to crumble.

"Brant?" He was pretty sure she was going to dangle a carrot in front of him, and that he was going to chomp on it.

"Hmm?"

"You need to say yes." Her eyes were a soft blue, her lips delectable.

"Why?"

"Because if you do this…" Her hands had slipped around his waist and he felt the last shred of his resolve caving in like a muddy embankment during a flood. "…I'll go on that honeymoon everyone's nagging us about."

Brant stared at her for a long moment. She was serious. A honeymoon.

He turned to Travis, his head swimming. "Looks like you need to send me the paperwork."

———

IT WAS Brant's night to cook, but he'd been out on a call that had taken three hours longer than it should have. Meaning he was late. Very late. He floored the truck, heading into Sweetheart Creek. The sheriff, seeing him coming, flashed his lights in warning. Brant hit the brakes, slowing to under the speed limit as he coasted into town. He gave Conroy Johnson a sheepish wave, and the man grinned back. He lowered his window and leaned out to talk.

Brant groaned to himself and slowed to a stop, putting down his own window. He'd texted April to let her know he was running late, but didn't want to try her patience this early in their marriage by stopping to gab with the sheriff. They were working on a routine where he'd come by after work and have supper, then spend the evening with her and Kurt. And before bed he'd head back to the ranch. In the mornings he'd do chores and meet April at the clinic if it was her day to work. It was nice, but he still couldn't wait for the day that he woke up beside her—or at least in the same house. He just had to hang in there a few more days and he'd soon be sharing the same roof. He'd already packed up most of his stuff, and Saturday morning—moving day—couldn't come soon enough.

"In a hurry to get home to the missus?"

Brant swallowed. If only he was in a rush the way the sheriff thought he was. "Sure am."

Johnson twisted his wrist, checking his watch. "Better hurry. You're gonna be late for supper." Before Brant could go, he said, "Here's a nickel's worth of free advice I give all new husbands. Ready for it?"

Brant nodded.

"Never be late for supper. Ever." His tone hinted at the wrath he must have faced from Mrs. Johnson early in his own marriage.

"Thanks for the warning."

"You're welcome. Now you'd best be getting along. Don't keep her waiting. Your mama raised her, and she's as likely to take you by the ear as Maria would."

Brant chuckled at the thought.

"Need any help moving on Saturday?"

"I think I'm about set, thanks." With a tip of his hat, Brant drove off. He took the second turn off Main and headed toward April's place, glad he'd soon be referring to it as home.

Travis had already sent him information on the college's study, and more sign-up paperwork than Brant had believed possible. He'd completed it all, meaning it was time to plan that honeymoon.

He parked in front of the house, hopped out and hurried up the front walk. He hit the doorbell before letting himself in.

"You don't have to ring the bell, silly," April said with a laugh, coming to greet him. He slipped an arm around her waist, then pulled her close for a hello kiss that quickly turned deeper and longer.

They really needed to take a honeymoon.

"Daddy Brant!" Kurt said, running to him, breaking up the kiss. Brant released April and bent to hug the little boy, who clung to him like a monkey as he straightened, lifting him in the process.

April faced Brant with crossed arms as he listened to an account of Kurt's day, finally lowering the boy, who ran off to play in his backyard fort under the floodlight Brant had set up for him.

"I thought you were cooking tonight?" April asked.

"I am." He glanced at the small clock she'd hung by the door. It was shaped like Kurt's favorite cartoon character, and for his benefit had sticky notes stuck to the hand positions for their morning departure time, to help Kurt arrive promptly at day care. Too bad it hadn't helped Brant arrive on time tonight.

April walked to him, slid her hands over his shoulders, plucked off his hat and then hung it on the hook beside the door. "Are you trying to get out of cooking?"

His palms found their favorite spot on her waist. "What do you say we head over to the diner?"

"You and I are eating out tomorrow night and the next night."

Date nights. Finally. It had been a busy week, but for whatever reason that had only served to make the days go by slower.

"Eat out!" Kurt hollered in excitement. He came sliding back into the entryway, scooting onto his butt. He had his cowboy boots on in record time, his purple unicorn from Carmichael tucked under his arm.

"I thought you were playing outside?" April asked him.

"I had to pee."

Brant raised his eyebrows at April with a smile and reached for his hat. "Looks like we're eating out tonight, too."

"This doesn't count as you cooking," April scolded lightly.

"Noted."

It was a warm January evening, and they walked the few blocks to the diner. By the time they arrived, Kurt had already decided on his order and announced it as soon as they were seated in a booth.

"I do like a man who can make up his mind," Mrs. Fisher said, after jotting it down. She focused on Brant and April, who were sitting across from each other, Kurt beside April. "Any word on where and when you're having your honeymoon?"

Brant looked to April, who shrugged. "Still open to ideas," he said.

"Hey, guys." Ryan slid into the booth next to him, elbowing him farther down the bench. "Mind if I join you?"

"Looks like you already did," Brant muttered, just before Mrs. Fisher took all their orders, then went to get their drinks.

"Uncle Ryan, how much does your dog weigh?" Kurt asked.

"Twenty-three pounds. How much do you weigh?"

"I don't know."

"Brant hasn't weighed you on his cow scale? He should. It's lots of fun."

Eyes wide, the little boy gazed across the table. "Can you weigh me on the cow scale?"

Brant pretended to measure him with his hands. "You might be heavy enough to tip the needle."

"It's digital," April said with a wry smile.

"What did I hear about a honeymoon?" Ryan interjected. "You have something planned?"

"They don't know where they're going," Mrs. Fisher said with a sigh as she set down their drinks. She shook her head and propped one hand on her hip. "Are you looking to go somewhere exotic or somewhere local?"

"It's up to April," Brant said.

She shrugged.

"You know," Ryan said thoughtfully, "the guy I know from working on that dating app was saying his wife's cottage is pretty romantic. Only problem is it's up in Canada. And it's winter. But he said it's remote and magical and all of that."

April and Brant glanced at each other, and she shrugged again.

"I bet he'd lend it to you for a few days." He lifted his hands and said, "What? I was talking about a little getaway for me and Carly. He offered up his place." Ryan's phone was at his ear before they could protest.

"There are a lot of nice honeymoon spots here in the state of Texas," Mrs. Fisher said, patting her teased hair. "You don't have to go to such expense. It's a honeymoon. It's not like you're going to be seeing any sights outside your room."

Brant choked and April blushed.

"What are you guys talking about?" Levi said, leaning over the back of the booth on April's side. Brant hadn't seen him come in, his cheeks rosy as though he'd been working outdoors all day.

"A honeymoon," Mrs. Fisher said. "I'm trying to convince them they don't need to break the bank."

"If you're flying somewhere, the ranch has a lot of points on its credit card right now. I've been using a few here and there while I try to keep up with Laura and all her business meetings for that perfume line of hers. If you pick a destination, just let me know and I'll get you some free flights."

"That would be great," Brant said.

"What's a honeymoon?" Kurt asked.

"It's a trip newlyweds go on after the wedding."

"Can I come?"

"Nope," Levi said.

"There was no wedding," Kurt said with a pout.

"There was. It just wasn't a big one with a party," April explained.

"Did Alexa and Polly talk to you about a date for the reception?" Mrs. Fisher said, referring to the Wylders' cousin Alexa McTavish, and their cousin Nick's girlfriend, Polly Morgan.

"A reception?" Brant looked at April. He'd thought that was optional.

"Couple of the Year," Mrs. Fisher reminded him with a frown.

"Oh, right," April said.

"Connor MacKenzie says we can use his cottage, but it's not fully winterized." Ryan had his over his phone. He removed it and asked Connor, "What exactly does that mean?" His nose wrinkled. "No plumbing." He was shaking his head. "Sorry, Connor. It sounds romantic and like a great getaway." He listened. "Helicopter?" He laughed. "No roads in. That's pretty cool and definitely private, but maybe not quite what my brother's looking for. Yes, maybe in the summer. Thanks anyway."

He ended the call and said, "No running water in the winter. They're working on winterizing Trixie Hollow, but it's over a hundred years old and a heritage building, so it's tough going. Maybe not your top choice for a honeymoon. Although the whole needing-to-share-body-heat-to-stay-warm might be up your alley…" He gave them a big grin.

Brant grinned back. "That's not a bad idea."

"Mom doesn't like being cold," Kurt said authoritatively, and April laughed.

"That's true," she said.

"So? Where do we go?" Brant asked her.

"How about something more local?"

"What's this? A family meeting?" Myles approached the booth, hand in hand with Karen Hartley, the local librarian.

"They need a honeymoon location," Mrs. Fisher said, still lingering. "They have a free flight anywhere, according to Levi, and they've already said no to a cottage in Canada with no plumbing. They need ideas."

Myles was quiet while Karen listed off a few tropical locations.

"I'm not sure I want to be that far away," April said, glancing toward Kurt.

"What about Blades?" Myles asked Ryan.

"Beach house!" Ryan said, pointing at him with both hands. "Yes!" He was on his phone again in a second.

"What's this?" Brant asked.

"Maverick Blades." Myles waited for Brant to remember. "From the NHL."

"Blades!" Brant said. "How's he doing?"

"Getting into trouble, by the sounds of things."

"From when you were kids and into hockey?" April asked. "The big guy?"

"That was so cute," Karen said. "I heard the story about you wanting to get into the NHL." She gave Myles an affectionate smile and snuggled against him.

"He has a new beach house in Galveston," Myles stated. "It's amazing." He kissed Karen, pulling her close.

"It's available," Ryan said, covering his phone with a hand again. "Tell him when you want it and it's yours."

"Next week," Brant said decisively.

"Next week," Ryan repeated into the phone. He gave Brant a nod.

It looked like his marriage was about to become more real with a honeymoon.

8

---

*B*rant walked the beach on Galveston Island with April. The Gulf of Mexico was cold, the breeze chilly, but it was still a gorgeous sunny January day. Maverick Blades's beach house was incredible, with floor-to-ceiling windows overlooking the water from every room on the east side. The furniture was comfortable, the fireplace grand and generous with its heat.

It was the perfect place for a three-day honeymoon, but instead of testing the various amenities, they were out walking the beach and settling into the idea of being on their honeymoon.

April picked up a shell, flipped it over, then tossed it into the water. Her pockets were clinking with shells and rocks she'd collected to bring back for Kurt. The boy had been elated to spend a few days with Maria and his uncles on the ranch. And April had been relieved to be only a short flight away—having opted to catch a flight from San Antonio to Houston rather than drive the five hours to the beach house.

"Getting hungry for supper?" Brant asked. They'd arrived around lunchtime, grabbing a sandwich in the airport before Maverick's assistant had appeared with a car for their personal use, insisting they take it for the duration of their stay.

It paid to have friends and family.

"What do you have in mind?" April asked.

"There's an amazing beachside restaurant a few miles from here. Very romantic. But after seeing Maverick's large deck, I was thinking maybe we could order in and enjoy it on our own private patio."

"Very romantic," she said, bowing slightly as though impressed. She pushed strands of hair off her face. She was smiling, happy, shy.

Their honeymoon was going to change things for them, and a part of Brant wanted to rush through the next three days to see where they ended up when they came out the other side.

April picked up a sand dollar, then returned to his side.

"Do you want a ring?" he asked, sliding their bare fingers together, interlocking their hands.

She shrugged. "It would probably get lost in your line of work. You'd be taking it off all the time."

"True. But do *you* want one?"

"My grandma gave me a ring years ago. I never wear it, but I like it. I could wear that."

"Is that what you want?"

She shrugged again and brushed his bare ring finger. "If it weren't for Old Man Lovely, how long do you think it would've taken us to get married?" There was an inquisitiveness in her gaze, brightening the amber flecks around her irises.

"A decade," he replied solemnly. They stopped walking and faced each other.

"Ten years?" She laughed, looking young and free, her dimples on full display. She gave him an affectionate push. "How could that be? You're the kind of man meant to be tied down. You're husband material."

Husband material. He'd heard that many times before, and he still wasn't sure if it was a compliment.

"I wasn't really on the market," he grumbled. "I still don't know how you lured me into marrying you. I'm a tough one to pin down, you know."

"Are you kidding?" Her smile was so big he could see her molars. "You practically smoked your tires, driving so fast to that chapel."

"Yes, but if we'd had to go through dating, an engagement and planning a wedding?" He drew out each word as though a traditional courtship with April would have been enduring a hardship. "You would've never got me down that aisle."

April rolled her eyes and leaned her shoulder against his as they began walking again. She smelled of sunshine and happiness.

"Is that true?" she asked after a moment.

He stopped and pushed his fingers through her windswept hair, combing it back from her face. "It's not." He met her calm gaze. "I've had a crush on you since the day Carmichael gave you that rodeo horse of yours. You were so happy, so full of life, so confident and bold. You've got this quick wit and sense of humor, but also a caring, sensitive side." He inhaled, then said on the exhale, "Irresistible."

It had never surprised him that Cole had gotten into so many fights while dating April on the rodeo circuit. She was the kind of woman every man wanted, and was well worth fighting for.

"I don't know if the woman you see is still here."

"She is." Strong, brave, determined to get what she wanted. He hadn't suggested she leave Heath, move towns or find a job. *She'd* decided. She'd known there was a better life for her, and she'd been the one to summon the courage to step outside of comfort and into the unknown. "But you're also more than that now, too."

"If that's a way of saying I've gained weight..." she grumbled, shifting from his side.

He tightened his grip. "I love your curves." He let a hand roam from her hip to her waist to her ribs. "Sexy and dangerous."

She gave him a patient, slightly more bashful smile.

"Truthfully, April, I didn't quite believe you were choosing me. That's why I sped to the chapel." He gently stroked her cheek. "I didn't want you to get away."

"Were you afraid someone else might snatch me up?" she teased, looking pleased.

"Yes."

"And are you rescuing me?" Her voice was soft and honest.

"Only your heart. The rest of that stuff you could do on your own."

"But I can't rescue my heart on my own?" She raised her chin, bringing her lips close to his.

"I don't think it would be the same." He rewarded her with a kiss that soon grew deeper, unraveling their tight grip on restraint and patience.

"I think we should go back to the beach house," April said, taking him by the hand.

If he'd been driving, he would have smoked his tires.

APRIL LAY NESTLED in Brant's arms, drowsy and contented. Their private view of the water from here in the master suite was something she never wanted to give up, never wanted to forget. Their extended weekend getaway was coming to an end tomorrow afternoon, but right now this moment was the only thing that felt real. Her job, the messy house with toys kicked underneath the couch, and even motherhood seemed distant.

Everything right here, right now, felt blissfully perfect.

She curled into Brant, sliding her left hand up his bare chest. Working with animals made him naturally strong and fit, his movements fluid and confident.

"I love being here," she murmured.

"It was a good idea, wasn't it?" Brant said, his voice low and rumbly. "When I'm buried up past my eyebrows in cattle because of that study, I'll be thinking of being here." He smiled down at her, looking tired but happy.

"We never did quite make it to the end of the beach or that restaurant, did we?"

He tightened his arms around her. "We found better things to do." He closed his eyes again, a smile still etched on his face.

"When we get back, are you moving into my bedroom?" she asked, toying with a small sprig of chest hair between his pecs. In a quest to take things slowly, Brant had been staying on the pullout couch at April's, but now the shift from "just friends" had been completed and there was no reason for them to sleep apart.

Originally, the idea of a honeymoon had left April skittish, her fears that they might not be compatible as anything more than friends giving her pause. But now she was glad she'd blurted out her honeymoon deal, grateful that Brant and the town had taken up the torch and made it happen.

"You know, we only made it to date night once," Brant said.

"What's your point?" she asked, disgruntled. She propped herself up on an elbow and tugged the sheet closer.

"Would that be rushing things?"

"We've just gone on a honeymoon and we're *married*." She gave him a funny look, unsure if he was teasing. "We're not rushing things."

"We eloped without even going out on a date," Brant said. He quirked his lips, looking pleased. "We went on a honeymoon before we dated, too. Nope, didn't rush a thing."

"So? Are you going to move into my room?"

He was quiet, his eyes closed, and for a moment she thought he was drifting off. Finally he said, "Sure. Why not?"

His casual tone made her huff in disgust. "You're awful, you know that?"

"You're the one who married me."

She huffed again. "You like being married to me."

"That's true, but there's no way you can prove it."

"Why would I need to?"

He was teasing her, in a carefree, affectionate way she wasn't used to. He was being confident, playful, sure. It was downright sexy.

"Brant?"

His eyes were still closed, that smile ever-present. "Hmm?"

"Do you—" She broke off abruptly.

One eye opened, then the other. He peered at her, his eyes so strikingly blue she almost couldn't believe they were real. "I do."

"But you don't know what I was going to say."

"Maybe," he said sleepily.

"What was I going to ask?" She laid her ear against his shoulder, her heart thrumming faster.

"If I loved you." His body was warm under hers, and the way she curved into him felt so good it was like they'd been made for this.

"And I do." He snugged her closer with a satisfied sigh, and she thought he might be falling asleep.

"Do you want to know if I do, too?"

"Sometimes you don't need words," he said. "Sometimes you just know."

BRANT SLIPPED onto a stool near the diner's kitchen, groaning inwardly when he realized he'd taken a seat beside his uncle Henry. He made a fleeting wish to be whisked back to Galveston with April.

"Hello, Uncle Henry," Brant said pleasantly. He lifted a finger, catching Mrs. Fisher's attention. "Coffee and an apple muffin, please."

"There's our newlywed." The waitress smiled, her eyes lighting up. "How's married life treating you so far? Good honeymoon in Galveston?"

Brant grinned. "Marriage is even better than I'd dreamed."

"You know she's just using you to get out of that marriage she never wanted," Henry grumbled.

Brant's spirits flagged. He was too exhausted from their quick honeymoon and its late nights, then jumping back into a full work week while still adjusting to family life—and Kurt's sudden need to sleep in their bed, tossing and kicking all night long—to deal with Henry and his moods. The honeymoon had left him energized and happy, but also tired. And wishing to go back again.

Mrs. Fisher had placed his cup of coffee in front of him, and he took a gulp so he wouldn't bite through his tongue while trying to hold it for his uncle's benefit.

"Oh, Henry," Jackie said, tapping him on the shoulder with a lacquered nail as she slipped onto the stool on his other side. "April loves Brant like crazy."

"She does?" Brant asked, unable to help himself. He'd seen in her eyes how she felt, but hadn't heard her say the words, leaving him with a sliver of doubt he couldn't quite disregard despite his gut feeling.

Jackie rolled her eyes. "You two haven't said it yet?" She shook her head and gave Mrs. Fisher a look that made the older woman laugh. "You guys don't do anything in order."

"That's what I've been telling April."

"That girl has always been scattered and impulsive," Henry said. "Just like her father."

"What's the special today?" Brant asked Mrs. Fisher, ignoring Henry so he wouldn't end up in a scuffle with the old man.

She gave him a dry look, one hand on her aproned waist. "The same it's been for the last fifteen years."

"What day is today?" Brant asked.

"She's already sucked the mind out of you," Henry grumbled bitterly.

"The honeymoon was that good?" Mrs. Fisher smirked, causing Jackie to giggle.

"Friday, right?" Brant stated. Glorious Friday. Date night and the weekend were calling him. "Give me the shepherd's pie."

"It's 9:30 a.m. *Thursday*, and you already ordered this." Mrs. Fisher placed a heated apple cinnamon muffin in front of him along with a pat of butter. She shook her head and exchanged another look with Jackie, adding, "The barn's booked for the reception, by the way."

"Already?" Brant asked.

She swatted the counter with a tea towel. "We don't slack on things like that."

"The last Saturday of the month," Jackie interjected. So eight days away. "The day after Cole's welcome back party."

Henry shook his head, a flyaway strand of white hair near the top of his head waving. "It won't happen."

"What won't?" Brant asked.

"The reception. Everyone knows you're just doing that fake-boyfriend thing you always do to help the ladies, so you can get a little something-something on the side."

Brant choked, and Mrs. Fisher gave a disapproving tsk.

"It's never been like that," Brant said darkly.

He opened his mouth to lay into his uncle, but Henry raised his voice as he said, "I ain't getting you a gift."

"That's fine." Brant stood.

"Their marriage is real," Jackie protested. "Have you not seen the way they look at each other?"

"I can't believe my brother raised such a group of fools," Henry replied, leaning to the side to fish his wallet out of his pocket.

Brant sat down again, then shoved a chunk of muffin in his mouth so his uncle could safely leave without getting a tongue-lashing.

"Fiona, you and I could run up to the chapel next year,"

Garfield Goodwin said, sliding onto Henry's stool as soon as he vacated it. Henry threw up his arms, his cheeks red.

"I haven't even paid yet and you're stealing my seat!"

Garfield ignored him, giving Mrs. Fisher a cheeky grin.

She scowled. "How many times do I have to tell you I'm a happily married woman?"

Jackie sucked in an audible breath at her fierce tone, shooting Brant a look.

"Can I get my bill?" he asked, chugging the last of his coffee. Mrs. Fisher refilled the cup as soon as he set it down, one hand on her hip as she continued to glower at Garfield.

"Well, the ol' memory isn't as good as it once was," the man drawled. "So I reckon you're gonna have to tell me quite a few times. Until I believe it."

Jackie leaned back behind Garfield and lowered her head. "Better pray for him, real quick," she muttered to Brant.

Elbow on the counter, he propped his forehead on his palm. Time to duck and cover, seeing as they couldn't safely flee.

When he finally hazarded a peek at Mrs. Fisher, she was giving Garfield a look so dark Brant feared for him. "Don't you talk like that, Mr. Garfield Goodwin. My marriage is none of your business. William and I have a relationship you will never understand."

As though realizing he had crossed the line, the man lifted his hands and lowered his gaze.

Mrs. Fisher laid into him, her voice loud enough for the whole diner to hear. "You should know me well enough to know that when I commit to someone, it's for the long haul. You gave up on Sally like an ice cream cone that fell on the sidewalk on a hot summer's day, but when I agree to for better or for worse, I'm keeping my word, even if some days it's a melted mess."

"I meant no harm, Fiona," Garfield said meekly.

"No matter what!" She thumped a fist on the counter, causing the line of coffee cups to jump. "You hear?"

"What I said was offside," Garfield mumbled.

"Completely out of line," Henry agreed, still lingering.

Brant glanced at his uncle with a warning shake of his head. At this point it was better to remain silent.

"I apologize from the bottom of my heart, and I will strive to do better," Garfield said humbly, then rose to his feet and left.

Mrs. Fisher gave a shaky sigh, as though brushing thoughts of the man from her mind, then began pouring coffee again, topping up everyone's cups. "True love isn't a whim. It's forever." Her mouth tightened with emotion and Brant's admiration for the woman rose substantially.

"Marriage is nothing but a bother," Henry retorted, sitting again.

Brant knew that was wrong. He was looking for what Mrs. Fisher had. Something more than a whim, that lasted over the long haul. For better or for worse.

HUMMING TO HIMSELF, Brant padded down the hallway toward the master bedroom in April's house. Kurt had fallen asleep in his own bed, midstory, and Brant was feeling optimistic about his own bedtime. He passed the bathroom and then backtracked. April was studiously staring at herself in the mirror, the kitchen scissors aimed at her bangs.

"What are you doing?" he asked, noting the drifts of brown hair surrounding her on the floor.

"Cutting my hair," she replied, not looking his way. She was holding her mouth at a funny angle, the scissors waving unsteadily as she tried to figure out which way to move them in the mirror's reversed image.

"Is this why your bangs are always crooked?" he asked in amusement. Was there anything this woman wasn't willing to try? She was either the bravest or craziest person he knew.

She lowered the scissors, looking at him. "They're not crooked." She turned back to the mirror, fingering various strands to check the fringe above her eyebrows, then let out a huff. "Well, they aren't bad, considering I cut them myself." She gave her head a shake, resettling her bangs, then raised the scissors again and took a few vertical snips.

"What are you doing?"

"Taking away some bluntness."

"You missed a chunk over here," he said, moving behind her. She smelled wonderful, and the nearness of her body was awakening his. With a lopsided grin, he pinched the lock between his fingers.

When April took aim with her scissors, he had an image of her taking off too much, so stepped between her and the mirror. "Let me."

She raised her eyebrows, but didn't relinquish the sheers. "What do you know about cutting hair?"

"That people shouldn't cut their own."

"Tons of people do."

"Yeah, semibald men. They take one of those razors and give themselves a buzz cut. It's a very attractive look for women, too," he said dryly.

"It saves me time and money," she protested.

"I don't think this is somewhere in life where it's worth saving time and money."

"You couldn't even tell I was cutting my own hair until you saw me in here."

"I just thought you'd spilled some awful gossip about Emma Sue down at the Big Hair Salon behind her back, and she was avenging herself by giving you crooked bangs."

April gave a pouty frown as though attempting to be mad. She was adorable, and Brant laughed, saying affectionately, "Come here."

She handed him the scissors and straightened her spine,

holding her head level. "Rescue me from crooked bangs, almighty man."

"This happens to be my specialty," Brant said calmly.

"Just remember I'm a human—your wife. Someone you want to be seen in public with, and not someone's shaggy mutt who's getting eye infections because their mangy mane keeps falling into their eyes."

Brant's right hand started to tremble, and he clutched it with his left, steadying the scissors. He performed life-and-death surgeries all the time. Cutting bangs wasn't high stakes. Although if he messed up his wife's hair, that could put the task on a similar scale.

"Trust me?" he asked, giving her a chance to back out.

"You're making me nervous. Just get to it."

"Here goes nothing." He carefully began snipping, taking off small bits at a time, trying to even the line of bangs by following her eyebrows. He studied his work. "I think your face is crooked."

He moved in for another snip and April laughed, shifting her head.

"Hold still!"

She quieted, her expression trusting, her smile relaxed. He wanted to kiss her, then lure her to the bedroom down the hall. Instead, he focused on her hair again, working at evening out the spots she'd missed. When he felt the job was done, he stepped out of the way so she could see herself in the mirror. "How's that?"

"Good," she said, looking pleased. "It's a bit blunt, though." She went to take the scissors from him, but he pulled them out of reach.

"I've got this."

He began imitating the vertical snipping motion he'd seen her do, loving how intimate this domestic moment felt. The effect was immediate, her bangs losing their sharp, straight line. It looked almost professional.

"This is much more fun than dealing with shaggy mutts, as you so eloquently put it."

He got bolder with the scissors, traveling from one side of her face to the other. It was trickier where her bangs met the rest of her luscious locks, the hair thicker. He took a brave snip and froze.

"What did you do?" April asked doubtfully, opening her eyes.

"Nothing."

She shoved him aside, staring at the mirror. "Seriously?" She gave him a dark, unimpressed look.

"I can fix it." He wasn't sure how you fixed taking out a chunk, but he was sure there was a way to cover it up until it grew out again. He pulled his phone from his back pocket. "I'll call Daisy-Mae."

April took his phone and slapped it down on the counter. "What makes you think she knows what to do? She isn't even a hairdresser."

"She won beauty pageants. I'm sure she knows everything there is to know about hair."

April scowled at him.

"Should I call Laura? Violet? Jackie?" He was getting desperate, but adding names to the list didn't seem to help her mood.

April wrangled the scissors from him and leaned over the sink, facing the mirror. She furiously fluffed her bangs and snipped, trying to make the missing chunk less obvious.

"Maybe you just need to wear a hat for the next few weeks," Brant suggested. It really wasn't that bad, now that she'd attacked the area. It was thinner than the other side, but not too noticeable.

He got another frown, but this one had a hint of amusement.

Forgiven.

His heart warmed.

"I could get you a razor," he teased, knowing he was pushing it, but that April wouldn't lash out. She'd turn this into a funny story, because that's what she did. She charged into things fearlessly, and if it all exploded, she just laughed, brushed off the dirt and walked away with some witty quip that made everyone chuckle. "You know, shave it all off and start fresh."

April let out a laugh full of incredulity. "Brant," she protested through her giggles. "You're awful! You did this on purpose so I'd go to a hairdresser, didn't you?"

"I swear I didn't!" He raised his hands as though she was going to arrest him.

"Maybe I should get even." She held the scissors like a weapon.

"I don't like this chunk here," he said, tugging at a random lock near the back of his head. "It likes to stick up after I've been wearing a hat."

"Perfect!" She made snipping motions with the scissors and he danced out of reach with a laugh.

Bits of hair fluttered off April from her haircut, and Brant reversed direction. Pinching the fabric of her shirt, he gave it a flick, sending more snippets flying."This blouse has got to go. You're going to track hair all through the house, and you know I just swept."

"Hmm. We can't make more work for my handsome husband." She reached for the hem and dragged it upward. As she tugged the shirt over her head, Brant wondered why he hadn't suggested it earlier.

9

"Brant got you this, too," Josh, the local courier, said, handing April his handheld device for her signature. He was grinning. Probably because the number of packages Brant had ordered for her since their honeymoon was keeping him gainfully employed.

"What is it?" She read the side of the box. A new bridle for her horse, Cookies. She sighed. It was as if Brant was taking care of every little thing she'd mentioned was bugging her over the past several weeks, from her worn bridle to the broken rearview mirror in her vehicle to her bangs. The haircut hadn't cost him anything, at least, and had turned out semi-decent despite the big chunk he'd accidentally snipped out.

She had already scrawled her signature to accept the package, but said to Josh, "I could've gotten one of these on my own."

He smiled and tipped his hat. "Ma'am, I think someone's just trying to show his affection."

She nodded with a sigh. "I know." And she couldn't fault Brant for caring. He was sweet, and it was in his nature to take care of people. Especially ones he felt needed help. And there was the problem. Their marriage hadn't evened out the balance in their relationship like she'd hoped. He was still rescuing her, but now it was from her everyday problems. If she wasn't careful, she'd depend on him too much, like she had with Heath. And in the end, that had left her with nothing.

She needed to set some boundaries and assert herself, assure Brant she could take care of herself, but that it might take more time than he wanted it to.

She took the box and marched to the back of the clinic to find Brant. Her husband was dozing in an easy chair, his large hands supporting a sleeping kitten tucked into his flannel snap-up jacket. He'd rescued the half-drowned, half-frozen feline from the recessed area around a water well head earlier in the day. Brant had returned from the call with the gray-and-white cat snuggled in his coat and a perturbed expression on his face. He'd closed himself in his office, on the phone with the county for almost an hour after that, April hearing the odd exclamation through his door about safety and banning those recessed well pits.

He looked so peaceful in the chair, and she knew he'd had a long, busy week with little sleep. But she needed to do this now, before she talked herself out of it.

"Brant?" April demanded, the box perched on her hip.

He opened his eyes and sat up, kicking the chair's footrest to lower it. Remembering the kitten, he curved a palm around its small body and stroked between its ears with a fingertip while easing back into a reclined position so as not to disturb it.

"What's up?" His expression softened as he looked at her, his sleepiness reminding her of mornings. Since he'd moved in, they'd fallen into an easy routine. In the mornings he would start the coffee, then bring her a cup as she showered, leaving it on the bathroom vanity. He would start prepping breakfast, occasionally disappearing if an emergency call drew him away, taking his dog, Dodge, with him.

He had no problems starting laundry, sweeping up crumbs

from under Kurt's chair and generally being an ideal husband. He was present in ways Heath had never been. Not even when they'd first married. The stark contrast reinforced her belief that she and Heath had never been right for each other.

"Everything okay?" Brant asked, peering at the box under her arm. Her annoyance about his pampering ebbed, since she knew he meant well.

"Sorry I woke you," she said. She tipped the box so he could read the label. "The bridle arrived. How much do I owe you for it?"

"What's mine is yours. And thanks for waking me up or I probably wouldn't sleep tonight."

"That's not a bad thing," she said with a wink. "It's date night, after all."

Last night, deep in their lovemaking, she had finally said it. Had finally told Brant she loved him. It had slipped out, and she worried it would be too easy for him to doubt her intent, to believe it had only been said in the heat of passion.

"Hey," she said lightly. "Have I ever told you I love you?"

His eyebrows flickered upward. "Planning on dying or something, MacFarlane?"

She heaved an impatient sigh and rolled her eyes. "Seriously, Wylder? I finally work up the courage to say it and you crack a joke?"

She spun on her heel and marched to the doorway, the burn of embarrassment singeing her cheeks and making her feel like a fool. Why couldn't she say "I love you" while looking him in the eye? Sure, she'd just told him she loved him, but it had felt like a roundabout observation rather than a proper declaration weighted with importance.

"Have I ever told you how much I love the sparkly doodads on the butt of your jeans?" he called after her, his tone teasing. "Especially when you're stomping away?"

Her footsteps faltered and she shook her head, evoking a chuckle from deep in his chest.

She turned in the doorway. "You're a real pain in the butt."

"A sparkly-doodad butt?" His eyes were dancing, his grin wide.

"Don't forget I'm off work at noon today," she said softly. He nodded. "And you need to stop buying me everything under the sun. You've already won me over."

"Have I?"

The question in his eyes at such a simple inquiry would haunt her for the rest of the day.

BRANT KNEW he'd gone too far buying the bridle for April. He could see it in her eyes when she'd stared down at him in the chair that morning. He'd been taking care of things for her because he loved her and knew she was pinched for money. But she might start to think he didn't believe she could take care of these things herself. Which wasn't true. There was simply a barrier in the way. A barrier he could remove while she worked up the courage to flat-out tell him she loved him, looking him in the eye as she did so.

He sat at the reception desk in the clinic, waiting for his regular receptionist, Lainie Hopewell, to arrive for her shift. April had the afternoon off, filling it with appointments around town for herself and Kurt. Brant had a few things to do out back, but they could wait. He'd learned in this business that if he had a chance to put his feet up, he should take it. There would always be enough work, if that's what he was looking for.

"Hi, Mr. Wylder," a female voice said from behind him.

Brant spun his chair around to face Robyn, the pregnant teenager who lived above the clinic in his old apartment, her parents having kicked her out when they'd heard she was expecting. Instead of rent, she did some light cleaning and restocking in the clinic after school. He double-checked the time. School wasn't due to let out for a few more hours.

"Hey, Robyn. How are you feeling?" She gave a feeble smile. "Shouldn't you be in class?"

"Too much morning sickness again." She sat in the extra office chair, her fingers tangled together in her lap.

"It's still bothering you?" She was in her second trimester, but the morning sickness didn't seem to want to abate.

"Yeah."

Robyn let out a shaky breath, and Brant moved to the water dispenser to fill a cup for her. She took it with a grateful smile.

"What's on your mind?"

"Blake and I want to move in together." Her boyfriend, a high school senior, had earned a college scholarship for his talents on the football field, and once the two of them were through the last few months of the twelfth grade, they'd be off on a new adventure.

"I don't mind if you both live in the apartment," Brant said.

"My parents want to sue Blake's family, and when we move in together, they might go all the way off the deep end." April had mentioned in passing that Robyn's parents wanted to go after Blake's family.

"Are you worried about your safety?" he asked gently, and her eyes widened with worry even though she shook her head.

"I don't want to drag you into this, Mr. Wylder. You've been really good to me. So has April."

He nodded, glad he and April could help. "I can handle difficult situations, Robyn," he told her. "Do what's best for you and the baby, okay? Don't worry about me."

"We're going to rent a mobile home near the swimming pool." She added quickly, "It's real cheap, and Blake has been working hard at two jobs."

Brant understood. April hadn't wanted handouts when she'd

moved out, either, even though she'd been in a similar bind, with no cash and no roof over her head. She'd been eager to get her boots back under her again, just like Robyn was.

"Know that the apartment is still an option if you two want it." He gestured to the suite above them. "But I also understand if you feel it's best to move out."

"We move into the trailer in a week. The landlord is letting us in a few days before the end of the month." She met Brant's eyes, revealing a spark of courage that made him smile. For all his worries, he knew she'd be okay. "But I was wondering if I could still work here. For pay."

He hadn't seen that coming. Robyn had been doing some light work, help he didn't actually need, seeing as he also had a cleaning company come in. But he'd wanted her to feel as though she was contributing toward her rent-free home. He'd already given April a job, one that made his life easier, but also wasn't truly needed. Could he afford to pay Robyn as well?

"Sure. Until you guys move away in the fall?"

She nodded, her eyes damp with gratitude.

"How many hours do you need?"

"Just part-time."

Her baby was due in the summer, and the couple had plans to move away at the end of August. He could make things work until then.

After Robyn left, Brant shook his head. He really was a rescuer, wasn't he?

As if reinforcing the answer, the gray-and-white tabby kitten meowed at him, wrapping himself around his ankles.

"What am I going to do with you? Hmm? Are you going to become a clinic kitty and live here, or can we find you a new home?" The well owner hadn't wanted the cat, claiming he'd never seen it before.

Brant picked up the feline, which he'd dubbed Tadpole, and set him on his favorite napping place, his chest. He leaned back in the office chair once more, mulling over his afternoon as the cat's rumbling purrs reverberated through him.

He slowly spun the chair to the right and carefully reached for the computer mouse to check the appointment calendar, eventually spying a blank stretch of time that afternoon. That didn't happen often. He could take care of a pretty big task if no emergencies came in.

He thumbed through the slips of paper left beside the phone in case some were for him. Most were reminders to call someone back, deal with an invoice and that sort of thing.

But the one at the bottom said " Find a place to board Cookies". April's horse. That beast was still at Heath's?

The divorce had been final for over a month, and Cookies was still on Heath's property. And being fed by him? No wonder the man wasn't paying April any child support.

Brant fingered the note. April loved that horse. Why would she leave him there when he could be at Sweet Meadows Ranch? Was she afraid to completely let go of her old marriage, the way she'd been afraid to sever ties with Cole?

Whatever hers reasoning, she wasn't planning to get Cookies today if she had filled her day with appointments.

Another barrier.

Well, he could take care of this one, and save her the hardship that would surely appear further down the line for letting Heath bear the expense of her horse. Boarding wasn't cheap, and he'd surely charge her for it.

Once Lainie arrived, Brant was out the door in record time, heading for Sweet Meadows Ranch to pick up the horse trailer.

He parked behind the stable, spying the trailer nearby, and had hopped out of his truck to adjust the hitch height when Betty Coulter, the riding stable manager, came toward him.

"Here's someone I haven't seen in a while," she said with a big smile. Her red-and-black-checkered shirt was tucked into a pair of jeans, her belt cinched tight around her middle.

"Hi, Betty," he said, giving her a quick hug. She was a no-nonsense woman with a heart of gold. Not just anyone could manage a program for special-needs riders like she did. His grandmother Ruth, who'd started the whole thing, would be proud of the work Betty did. "Has April talked to you about Cookies?"

"We spoke about him joining the riding program a few weeks back, and she seemed game. But so far, no horse." If Brant wasn't mistaken, there was a flicker of concern in Betty's eyes.

"How about today?"

"I sure could use another ride for the kids. Laura's scholarships have drawn a lot of attention and we're at full capacity. Cookies is well-trained and old enough now that he won't rile up the others. He used to like to prove himself, if I recall. But he was just a few years old back then, and now I hear he's nearly retired and mellow." She winked. "Like me."

Brant let out a bark of laughter, and Betty grinned.

"I'll go collect him then."

"You can put him in the empty stall on the east end. I'll get some feed and water ready. Do you need help hooking up the trailer?"

"I've got it, thanks. The new clinic truck has a backup camera."

"Well, I guess I'm redundant," the woman said amicably, as she slapped her hands on her thighs, releasing a cloud of dust.

"They keep telling us technology's going to take over the world," Brant said easily, climbing into his truck.

"Then I guess today's the day. Mark it in the history books."

Brant backed up to the horse trailer, then hitched it on. Before he left the yard, he sent April a quick text, letting her know he was picking up Cookies. Then he headed to the one property he had hoped he would never have to set foot on again.

"BRANT? WHAT ARE YOU DOING?" April panted, running to catch up with him behind the Sweet Meadows Ranch riding stable.

She'd left Kurt in the kitchen with Maria, who was teaching him how to make lasagna. After their last appointment of the day, April and Kurt had stopped by the ranch, where she had planned to confirm with Maria and Betty that her horse, Cookies, could stay here. She wanted to iron out the details of him being used in the children's riding program in exchange for his upkeep. She'd intended to get that sorted out, and then tomorrow, while Heath was still away, retrieve her horse.

She'd been chatting in the kitchen about her day, working her way up to the topic of her horse, when she'd felt tingles up her spine. Then, through the patio window, she'd caught a glimpse of Brant's clinic truck pulling a horse trailer, heading for the stables.

Instantly, she'd known.

She'd excused herself and slipped out the back door. By the time she got to him, Brant was already opening the trailer doors, revealing her black-and-white horse, wearing the new bridle she'd left behind the reception desk at work.

Cookies huffed happily and trotted over to her. She stroked his long nose, feeling guilty for not spending enough time with him over the past several years, and particularly the last few months. They used to spend hours together every day, and she suspected he missed her as much as she missed him. She nuzzled him back, knowing that the Sweet Meadows Ranch riders would give him the attention he deserved.

But she'd planned to bring him here herself.

She turned to Brant.

"I saw your note, and had some free time this afternoon," Brant said casually. He was watching her from under the brim of his hat, waiting for her reaction.

"Do you think maybe you should have asked first?"

"I sent you a text."

"My charging cord stopped working. And besides, this isn't a text-and-go kind of thing. This is a *conversation* kind of thing."

"Betty said you'd discussed it." His eyes shifted away.

"And did she also mention that we didn't have any details sorted out? Or that I hadn't yet run it by the owners of the ranch?"

"You're married to me. This is your ranch, too. Your home."

She sighed, knowing that wasn't totally true. She couldn't make assumptions when it came to making any kind of change. And boarding a horse here was a change, even if Cookies earned his keep.

Plus she'd been avoiding Heath and discussing her marital status with him. And now her horse was gone from his property while he was away, as if she was afraid to see him. She'd planned to talk to him first, be up-front. And yes, she'd put it off for a long time, but was working toward dealing with it at her own pace.

Brant rubbed the back of his neck, then eased the trailer doors closed.

"Brant." She waited for him to turn to her. "Cookies is why I'm here. I'm taking care of this. I was just working out an agreement with your mom, Levi and Betty, since they're running the riding program and Cookies is going to participate. Then tonight I was going to call Heath, and on the weekend get Cookies."

"Thought I was helping," he muttered, giving the doors a shake to ensure they were properly closed.

"No, you were trying to save me."

He slowly lowered his hands and turned to her. "You believe I think you aren't capable of taking care of your own business?" His eyes sought hers. "April, I'm your husband. I'm going to help. I'm going to take care of things for you. We're partners."

The honest sincerity in his expression had her anger crumbling along with her sense of righteous indignation.

He was doing this because he loved her. This was normal

behavior. He wasn't trying to take away her sense of independence. So why did she feel that way?

Because it seemed all she was doing was taking and not giving back, and she'd been raised to be independent and helpful.

She steepled her hands in front of her mouth and calmed herself. "I'm sorry. Maybe I'm still sensitive about the idea that your help is a form of rescue, and that none of this is real." Her voice shook, and she couldn't make eye contact. When her hands started fluttering she jammed them into her jeans pockets, then pulled them out and hugged herself. Why was she acting like she was vulnerable over something so minor and sweet? This man knew she was capable and competent. He'd grown up with her. He was acting out of love.

Brant eased his way to her side and slipped his hands around her waist. Cookies nudged his hat with his nose, as though saying all was forgiven.

Brant smiled and readjusted his hat. "I forgot what a rotter this one is." He gave Cookies an affectionate pat on the neck.

"It's why the two of us get along so well," April said.

Brant chuckled and pulled her in for a long, soulful kiss that made everything in her world feel perfectly right once again.

April looked at the steaming cup of coffee waiting for her on the bathroom vanity as she toweled her hair dry on Monday morning, and smiled at Brant's thoughtfulness. She took a sip, thinking of all the things he'd done for her over the past week since their honeymoon. It was a lot, and she wondered if he was going to hit a wall from trying to do it all.

They'd been sticking to their two-date-nights a week, and each morning Brant would roll out of bed and do his chores on the family ranch, then come home again for breakfast before heading to the clinic. Never mind the extra work he had with his animal control job and the college's study. The man was doing too much, and April feared he was going to burn out. Last night he'd fallen into bed exhausted, and was asleep before he'd even taken his socks off.

She smiled, thinking of a few reasons he'd been wiped out. They weren't all bad. But he was doing a lot of things for her he didn't need to. She'd grown up elbow to elbow with the Wylder boys on the ranch, chipping in like part of the family.

And when she hadn't been with them, she'd been in that quiet little house on the next quarter section over, figuring out how to do laundry for herself and her father, cooking, cleaning, and holding herself accountable for getting her homework done.

It was time to dig in and stand beside Brant, shouldering the weight alongside him. She just needed a plan to help speed things along.

Wrapped in her bath towel, she strolled into the bedroom, the smell of Brant's aftershave making her smile. She rifled through her bedstand drawer, found a pen and notepad, and began making a list, clutching the towel when it started to slip off.

Take over Brant's share of cooking nights.

The man was already doing so much, the least she could do would be take care of more things around the house, even though he'd insisted on going halfsies with housework. They could always readdress that later in their relationship.

She tapped her pen on the pad, thinking.

Tell Heath I remarried.

She shuddered. She hadn't called him like she'd planned. He'd likely already heard, but she wanted to be up front and honest with him in hopes he'd be the same, and she felt he deserved to hear the truth straight from her.

Look into how remarrying changes our divorce agreements, then talk to him.

Heath wasn't going to be less financially responsible for Kurt now, but he might feel he should be. He might have to pay her less alimony, though. Either way, if things continued to remain topsy-turvy with her ex, it meant she was going to have to rely on Brant even more for her and Kurt's care.

She hadn't married Brant so he could solve her problems, and right now, if anything happened to him, she'd be in a devastating financial position, just like she had when she'd left Heath. She needed to ensure she took care of herself—even though she was confident she and Brant were in it for the long haul—because that would mean taking care of Kurt and Brant, too.

Get a job outside of the clinic.

She frowned at the words she'd written. She enjoyed working with Brant. She savored their morning coffee in the back of the office, the stolen kisses throughout the day, the flexible schedule and the work, as well.

But she knew the position was one Brant had stretched the clinic budget to create, so that she'd have a job. And she'd seen the tightness of his mouth when he'd told her Robyn was moving out of the apartment and wanted to work for him part-time, as a paid employee. Giving the teen a place to stay hadn't cost him anything, but a part-time job would.

Call Jenny Oliver about a job.

April paused for a second, tapping the pen against her lips. It wasn't just the big things that would help her and Brant, though. The small things wore on a person, too.

Brant liked taking care of people, but couldn't she have found the five minutes needed to buy glue for her rearview mirror? Then another five to adhere it to her windshield? He'd ordered her the new bridle, bought Kurt new shoes a few days after he'd complained about his old ones being tight, while she'd been busy texting Heath, asking where the child support payment was. Yes, Brant was good at beating her to the punch when it came to fixing problems, but she could improve her speed.

Take care of more details—faster.

The problem was money. She couldn't always immediately afford to take care of details like glue, shoes and lawyers. Brant had made it clear that what was his was hers, and she had said the same, but then realized she had nothing. Everything she had came from Brant, whether it was her paycheck or the roof over her head. If she was going to contribute, she needed to take action.

Determined to start, she picked up her phone and dialed Jenny Oliver to see if a job at Blue Tumbleweed had come open.

BRANT STOPPED JUST before he reached the doorway of the diner, frowning. He backtracked a few paces and glanced through the large picture window of Jenny Oliver's store, Blue Tumbleweed. Beyond the display of dazzling cowboy boots, suede jackets and new Western blouses was a woman who caught his attention no matter where he went or what he was doing.

April MacFarlane.

His wife.

Also his part-time receptionist who didn't have a shift today.

She was holding up several shirts for MayBeth Albright to peruse. The middle-aged woman shook her head, and April put them back on the rack before bringing out another one.

He knew April. He knew MayBeth. And the two of them did not shop together.

Which meant April worked for Jenny?

Since when?

He pushed open the door and stepped inside the shop. It smelled of leather, new clothes and an essential oil he couldn't name.

April was hustling around a rack, saying to MayBeth, "Hang on, I think we have a small one over here."

"April?" he said.

She broke stride, her mouth dropping open as though she was guilty of something. "Brant. Hi."

He came closer, keeping his voice low. "You work here?"

Her face immediately flushed. "Jenny needed some help."

"For today?"

She shook her head, and he nodded as though he understood the fact that she was working at a new job on her day off, and hadn't mentioned it to him.

April slipped the blouse she was holding into a rack of denim jackets. "And I was kind of thinking…" Her shoulders hunched.

Brant pulled the shirt out and handed it back to her. "Doesn't go there."

She clutched the hanger with both hands. "Maybe it would be best if I didn't work for you?"

He'd never seen her tentative like this. He'd also never seen this coming. Not even a hint. And he was living with the woman. He was married to her.

"Am I not paying you enough? Do you need more flexibility in your hours? Is it about Lainie? I know she can get feisty about where people put things in the fridge, but we can't take her personally. I like working with you."

Brant dragged a hand over his face, trying to think what this secret job might mean. It felt like that situation with Shelley. As she'd gotten her feet under her, she'd taken on new things. He'd been proud. But then she'd grown more and more distant, as well as secretive. Then she'd left.

Was April on the same path?

Brant wanted what April wanted, and she desired independence, but he couldn't ignore how this new job was making his gut scream "Danger!"

"I like working with you, too," April said, placing a hand on his arm. He flinched, as the tone she was using reminded him of breakups.

"Then what is it?" he asked, his voice almost a growl.

"I need a life that's mine."

Was she kidding him? They were married. Why would she feel the need to have a separate life, or a job away from him, unless she wanted to *be* away from him?

She'd been upset when he'd brought Cookies to the Sweet Meadows Ranch, just like she'd been frustrated with his gifts. He'd handled that, but this amount of rejection was starting to feel personal.

"My life is your life. Without you, I don't have one," she was saying.

"We're married," he answered, the words catching in his throat.

"I know, but I just feel…" She closed her eyes as though struggling to find the right thing to say, or maybe for the strength to express what he didn't want to hear.

"…Feel like you don't want to see me that much," he said, completing her sentence for her.

Her eyes flew wide. "No! It's not that."

"Do you have it in medium?" MayBeth called out.

"Sorry, I need a second," April called back to her, and the woman let out a huff of disapproval.

"I think we need more than a second."

April's eyes flashed with impatience. "I need to have my own money. Not money I'm taking from your clinic."

"You're earning it."

"In a job you made up for me."

Brant shoved his hat back on his head, a need to yell and throw something growing within him. "And you resent me for that?"

Why did she have such a problem with him being a loving, helpful husband? He wasn't like the other men she'd been with. He wasn't playing games or trying to wind her up or get her to live his life. He was trying to help her by clearing things out of her way so she could do what was important. How was that a problem?

Her eyes were pleading with him for understanding.

"We couldn't discuss this before you decided you needed to leave?"

"I'm not leaving."

"It sounds like you're leaving the clinic."

"Well… I am, but…"

"You're leaving." He shifted from foot to foot, crossing his arms. "What's next?"

"Nothing is next. Brant, you can't afford me working at the clinic."

"Maybe I can."

"You can't. Not both me and Robyn."

"So you made the unilateral choice. You think you know what's best for me and my clinic?"

"You made the choice to move my horse without talking to me."

"Your horse was still at your ex-husband's house!"

"And Cookies was fine there!"

"You know Heath's going to hold that against you."

"I was dealing with it."

"Like you were dealing with leaving him? It took you two years, April. Two. Years."

Her eyes shut as though blocking out the verbal blow, and he turned away, frustrated with himself.

She'd first expressed her desire to leave Heath two years ago, but didn't have the resources. Brant had told her she could move back to the ranch, but her pride had kept her from agreeing.

He'd let it go until she'd brought it up again at the end of last summer. He'd bought Luanne Blackburn's house from Laura so April would have somewhere to go when she was ready, and he'd let her know she could work for him.

He'd thought he'd let her make her own choice to leave. But maybe she'd wanted to stay. Maybe that was why she'd balked when he'd bought the house, offering her free rent until she could manage it on her own. Maybe that was why she'd left Cookies on the farm. Maybe it wasn't actually about independence and contributing, like she'd said.

"Have you told him we're married?" he asked.

She inhaled so slowly he knew the answer was no.

"I need to stand on my own two feet," she said evenly. "What if something happens to you, and I can't take care of myself and my son? Then what?"

Brant turned, walking to the door on stiff legs, unable to think, feel or breathe.

"Hey, we're having that welcome-back party for Cole tonight," Myles said. "You coming?"

Brant blinked at his brother, trying to fight off the exhaustion that clung to him, so he could focus. "What?" The kitten on his chest stretched and Brant sat up in his clinic's armchair, setting the cat on the floor. He must have dozed off here once he'd finished the day's files, Myles letting himself in the back with the security code. "What time is it?"

"Eight." His brother gestured toward the rear door. "It's at the Watering Hole. We can walk over."

"Why?"

"Because Cole came back and we want him to feel welcome," Myles said slowly. "Are you okay?"

"Yeah, sure." Brant blinked a few times and shook his head, trying to clear his mind. Somehow it was already Friday night, which meant tomorrow was his and April's wedding reception. He rubbed his jaw, realizing he hadn't shaved that morning.

"How about you and April? You two doing okay?"

"Fine." Brant got up, and Tadpole jumped onto the chair's warm spot.

"I heard you missed date night tonight."

"It's been a busy week."

"You sure it's not about that fight you and April had in Blue Tumbleweed on Monday?"

Brant tipped his head back and groaned. He'd spent way too much time agonizing over that argument, and how April had pulled the rug out from under him with her secret job. They were married. She should feel she could tell him stuff like that. But she couldn't even summon the courage to say she loved him unless they were...

He rubbed his eyes, muttering, "Is word of our fight all over town?"

"Of course."

Sweetheart Creek. What a pain in the butt.

"What time is the party?"

"Now."

Brant glanced around for his jacket.

"Is April coming?" Myles asked.

"She's taking a lot of shifts for Jenny," he muttered, knowing that some of those shifts were to get her away from home—and him. Just like he'd checked on some herds ahead of schedule for the college study.

"Jenny's is closed for the night."

"Oh, right." Brant stretched, reality pressing in on him. "How did I forget about this party?" He checked his pockets for his wallet and phone.

"You've been distracted," Myles said with a lopsided grin. "You sure you and April are okay?"

"Of course." He'd barely seen her all week, which meant they hadn't been actively fighting. But it also meant they hadn't resolved anything.

In fact, Brant was afraid to talk to April. He feared she might spill the truth on why she'd married him. And if he didn't know the truth, he could hold on to the fantasy for just a little longer.

"That's not nearly cute enough," Jackie protested, when April strode into her living room, ready to go to Cole's welcome-back party. She was in everyday jeans and a pale blue sweater, her hair in a ponytail. Whereas Jackie was in tight jeans, a slinky off-the-shoulder knitted top and high heels.

"I don't need to look cute. He's my ex-boyfriend, and I'm married."

"Where is that husband of yours, anyway?" Jackie asked,

looking around the living room as though expecting Brant to appear.

"And where is Heath?" April replied, checking the clock by the door. He'd said he would arrive before Kurt's bedtime, and that was only five minutes away. Kurt was already in bed, story chosen, teeth brushed, eagerly waiting for his father after weeks of broken promises.

She'd finally called Heath and told him she was married, that she'd retrieved Cookies and that it was time for them to get serious about following their post-divorce agreements. He'd concurred and said he'd take care of Kurt tonight so she could go out.

"Heath?" Jackie repeated, a note of incredulity in her tone.

"That's right," April said steadily.

"*Why?*"

"He's babysitting Kurt."

"It's not his week to have him."

Technically, it was, but April hoped tonight would be the first step in the two of them getting things on track. Heath agreeing to take care of Kurt was a win, and if she could ease him into adhering to their agreement little by little, without having a tremendous fight that set them back, they'd get a lot further faster. She just hoped he hadn't said yes to tonight so he'd have a reason to pop by and yell at her for moving on. It was tough enough dealing with an upset Brant.

"So Heath's coming here?" Jackie asked, her tone flat and expressionless now. She inhaled with a huff, as though she'd heard something she didn't feel good about.

"Yes," April said, checking her pale lipstick in the entry's mirror.

The doorbell rang, and Jackie let out a long sigh. "I'll wait outside." She opened the door, giving Heath a tight smile. He looked large and uncomfortable standing on the front step, and had bags under his eyes. Jackie stepped past him and he came inside.

"Hey," April said. "Bedtime is—"

"Seven-thirty," Heath said automatically. He hadn't moved from the doorway, his gaze locked on her. "You married him."

April stilled. "I did," she said evenly. "Kurt will keep your last name, and I'll continue to keep my maiden name." Like she always had.

"You plan to leave him, too, then?"

"No," she said firmly, her anger mounting.

Heath was strangely subdued, and she wasn't sure if he was inwardly building toward a sudden burst of yelling or not. She felt as though *she* was ready to fight, that was for sure.

They stared at each other for a long moment, then Heath took a tentative step toward her, and suddenly she was in his arms, receiving a hug that made it hard to breathe.

"Heath?" She tapped his shoulder. He released her. "I have to go."

"I'll try better," he whispered, his eyes dark with something she couldn't pinpoint.

"I'll be back at nine," she said, hurrying out the door, unsure what was going through her ex's mind.

"Have fun tonight," Heath said, leaning against the doorjamb, his voice thick but calm.

April didn't reply, her heart racing with uncertainty. She closed the door behind her and inhaled a soothing lungful of evening air. That had been weird, as well as way too mature for either of them.

"No yelling?" Jackie asked, her arms crossed. She was waiting by her car, eyes narrowed.

"Let's walk."

"It's cold and I'm wearing these stupid high heels, not boots like you."

"I'm walking." April needed to reset her mind and mood

before she saw Brant at the Watering Hole—assuming he even came.

"Fine." Jackie fell into step beside her, leaving her sports car parked in front of April's. Nothing in town was more than a dozen blocks away, and the saloon was only four from here.

After half a block, Jackie asked, "Do you miss him?"

"He's been working a lot."

"Are we talking about Heath or Brant?"

"What?"

"Why did you leave your horse with him? Cookies is like your second child."

April's shoulders sagged. "What else was I going to do? I can't afford a horse right now."

"Is that all it was?" Jackie stopped at the curb, under a streetlight. They were still a few blocks from the saloon, with no traffic in sight.

"Why did you stop?" April gestured to the road.

"Do you still love Heath?"

"We never loved each other." The way she'd felt about him was nothing compared to how she felt about Brant.

"Then?"

"What are you getting at?" April asked, turning to face her friend.

Jackie began walking again, her high heels tapping on the asphalt as she crossed the intersection. She made jeans and heels look sexy, and April wondered if the outfit was intentionally chosen to help her stand out tonight and catch a certain someone's attention.

"Where's Brant? Is he meeting you there?"

"I don't know." The mascara April had swiped over her lashes felt heavy, as did her heart. Brant hadn't taken her recent job change very well. She was still working at the clinic—and yet hardly ever seeing Brant there—as well as at Jenny's, and it felt like most of her week's earnings would be going toward day care.

But she was contributing to the household, not by taking money from Brant's clinic just to give it back to him, but from somewhere else. And that felt good.

Brant's reaction, however, didn't feel good. When she'd called Jenny on Monday morning, April had been told she could start immediately. So she had. She'd planned to tell Brant about the new job at supper, but he'd found her in the boutique first. All week they'd avoided each other, the tension growing thick at home. In fact, he was barely there anymore, with emergency after emergency sweeping him away. She'd even checked up on him once, phoning the ranch he said he'd been called to. He was there. The emergency real.

She was growing paranoid, but neither of them was willing to admit to the wedge that seemed to slide further and further between them this week. It was worse than fighting. At least with a fight you got to air your grievances and maybe try to solve them.

Instead, he was simply absent, avoiding her so he could avoid the issue. He'd even blown off date night without so much as a word. That had really left her feeling shaky inside.

"Are you okay?" Jackie asked, and April nodded. "I don't think you are."

"It's just been a tough week, that's all."

"There've been a lot of adjustments in your life lately," she said sympathetically. "You know, emotion-wise. As well as with work and at home…"

April nodded again, her eyes threatening to well up and betray the I'm-okay vibe she was trying to put out there. She'd expected her friend to crack a joke to lighten the mood, but instead she was being so empathetic it made April want to sit down on the curb and bawl.

"Hey, so big party tonight," April said, determined to change the mood of their conversation, as well as the topic. "Cole's still single, isn't he?" She hadn't heard any rumors about him seeing anyone in the five weeks he'd been home.

Jackie began walking faster.

"Are you chicken?" April chirped, catching up with her. Jackie wasn't smiling and April frowned, confused by the way she was acting tonight.

"He's not my type."

"He's a Wylder. They're *all* your type. Plus you've been waiting for Cole since forever."

"I'm not looking for a fling."

"You know I don't care if you go after him."

"Thanks, but I'm not interested."

"In fact, I think you guys would make a great couple."

"Why? Because I can't keep a man longer than a few months, and he's the one they say puts the 'wild' in Wylder?"

"No, because you're both fun people," April said, unable to come to grips with this change in Jackie. She'd been pining after Cole for eons. Why wouldn't she go for him now that he was home and unattached? "I think you should kiss him tonight and see what happens." She nudged her friend, trying to get her to smile and act more like herself.

"Are we giving each other love advice?" Jackie asked, turning abruptly. Her dark expression stopped April cold.

"Um..."

"You know any woman in town would be happy to have a man like Brant. He loves you. Just you. And you're letting stupid stuff get in the way. He chose you. Try running with that instead of finding reasons not to."

"But we're..." April was shaking her head, unsure how to reply.

"You don't even know where your husband is tonight. You've been married for less than a month, not twenty years. A week ago you were on your honeymoon."

"We're just busy," April lied, feeling the lameness of the

excuse. "And I've been trying to get a bit of independence, so my entire life doesn't hinge on his, and he took it personally. He's trying to rescue me, which is really sweet, but it's not what I need. I need him to love me even if I'm a mess."

Jackie let out a frustrated groan. "There has never been a time in your whole life that you needed rescuing, April MacFarlane. Sometimes you take the chicken's way out, such as marrying Heath."

"That wasn't the chicken's—"

"Did you feel *he* was rescuing you, too?"

April sputtered. "No."

"Exactly. Know why? Because you don't need to be rescued. And you never have." When April opened her mouth to protest, Jackie demanded, "Who taught you to do laundry and cook and clean for you and your dad?"

"Nobody." Maria had given her tips and suggestions after she'd learned April was doing it all herself.

"Because you figured it out on your own. So cut the crap and give up the excuses, since marriage is something you could figure out if you weren't afraid to."

Jackie turned and started striding down the sidewalk again.

April gaped after her for a beat, then hurried to catch up. She fell into stride beside her, silent for several moments. "But it's just that he's taking care of *everything*," she finally said. How did she work around that? He'd been so hurt to find her taking on a new job, and unwilling to see the reasons it would help both of them.

"Seriously? Quit it. Just…" Jackie inhaled, staring up into the sky, her eyes damp. "Quit undermining what you have."

April blinked as though her friend had slapped her. "What's gotten into you?"

"It's hard watching you take love for granted again and again and again."

"I'm not."

"How many serious relationships have you had in the—"

Jackie halted abruptly and let out a shaky sigh, as though controlling her anger and frustration. "Never mind. I don't want to fight with you."

But April knew where her friend was going, even if she hadn't said it. April had popped in and out of three serious relationships over the past six years. Meanwhile, Jackie had had zero. She'd been out having fun, not dealing with complicated emotional messes.

"You're not perfect when it comes to this stuff, either," April said softly. "Milk lasts longer than your best relationships."

Now Jackie looked as though she'd been slapped, and April realized she'd overstepped.

"All I'm saying is that maybe you need to get over your fears and kiss Cole," she said lightly. "Maybe there's something there."

"So go have a fling and forget about looking for love?" Jackie muttered, her tone hinting at danger. "Because why would flirty, fun Jackie Moorhouse ever want anything serious when she's obviously so happy with her dairy-length relationships?"

"No, I meant…" When Jackie said it like that, it felt empty and sad. Lonely, too. "I mean, love will happen. Right? But why not have some fun while you wait?"

"I forgot. Love comes by every few years. I'll just fill the time in between with some meaningless flings. And if I find a guy, but it looks like a relationship might be too much work, I'll ditch him and wait for the next man to come along who's willing to fight over me."

"That's not what I mean."

"Then what is it? You get all the men falling over you with their hearts served up on a platter, and I get the flings? You get to complain, but I don't?" Jackie gave a tight shake of her head and strode ahead, jaywalking and leaving April behind.

"Jackie, I'm sorry."

Her friend hunched her shoulders in her jacket, muttering, "Save it."

April blinked back tears, confused by Jackie's outburst. She'd been trying to encourage her, not rub her marriage in Jackie's face. Because why would she? It was a painful mess, and in some ways Jackie's simple, uncomplicated life was enviable.

As April hit Main Street on her own, Bill the armadillo came out of the shadows and growled at her. She stomped her feet and waved her hands, letting out a ferocious roar that hurt her throat. The beast scrambled backward, darting down a narrow alley between two buildings.

She wished all the beasts in her life were that easy to frighten away.

There she was. April was wearing jeans and a sweater, looking casual and comfortable, and as gorgeous as always despite the deep furrow between her brows. Brant began weaving between partygoers in the Watering Hole, heading her way.

He was just about to reach her when Cole stepped into his line of sight, blocking his view. His brother said something to April that made her laugh, her frown vanishing. Then his palm was on her waist, his left hand in her right, and they were dancing.

Brant closed his fists.

He began elbowing toward them as they danced away. The last thing he needed right now was for Cole to come zipping into April's life and convincing her that being married wasn't for her. She wasn't in the best head space, given all their fighting, and he needed to show her he had no ulterior motives for being a good, loving husband. He needed her to see that before she left him for real. And her laughing with Cole wouldn't help. Not tonight.

Myles caught his arm. "Hey there, Brant. Where are you going looking like you want to stick a shiv in someone's throat?" His brother's tone was mild, but his words struck home.

Brant forced himself to inhale, then exhale the rage that had built up in short order. He was going to need to exhale for about a year or two the way jealousy was clouding his mind, tightening the muscles in his face until he felt as though his head was going to split in two.

"Let's go outside," Myles suggested.

Brant's hands bunched again. "No."

"I'm serious." Myles clutched his biceps and bodily removed him from the saloon, smiling and giving everyone they passed an easy, confident hello.

"You need to get ahold of yourself," Myles said in his ear as he pushed him outside. "Whatever's going on between you and April, you need to leave it at the door. She's allowed to dance with our brother at his party. You hear?"

Brant fumed. Of course she was allowed to dance with him, but that didn't mean he had to like it.

"People are already talking about you guys. People respect you, but if you act on whatever's going through your head, you're going to lose that as well as your business. Maybe even April. You hear me?" He gave Brant a shake.

Brant slapped his brother's hands away and scowled. "What are they saying?"

"I've seen this look in your eyes before."

He was referring to the night Brant had fought with Cole, the last day their brother had spent on the ranch, five years ago.

The strength of Brant's anger faded.

"This is different," he muttered, knowing his argument was groundless.

"Is it? Because you're acting like a jealous caveman. Being angry and righteous won't make anyone behave the way you feel is right. Trust her."

"She thinks I'm rescuing her. She took a job at Jenny's and

already has one foot out the door." He had to pace the sidewalk, the feeling in his gut leaving him unsettled. "She didn't want me getting her horse from Heath." He met Myles's eye on that one. "She wanted to leave Cookies with him, not bring him to our ranch. What am I supposed to think?"

"Do you love her?"

Brant refused to speak.

"You know she loves you?"

He feared it wasn't in the way that would get them through the long haul Mrs. Fisher had referred to in the diner the other day.

"What she's saying and what she's doing are two separate things," Brant said. "What am I supposed to believe?"

"You've swept in like a knight on a white horse."

Brant glowered at his brother's assessment.

"Maybe she needs to take care of some of this stuff for closure, so she can feel like a competent, independent human being. Maybe she wants to feel control over her life and like she can take care of her son."

But she wasn't taking care of things. She was floundering, hitting barriers.

"I can take care of her and Kurt."

"She knows that. But maybe she needs to feel like it. Even just a little bit. Isn't that why she left Heath? She was living his life, not her own?"

April's statement from Monday hit him in the solar plexus.

"My life is your life. Without you, I don't have one."

He'd excused her words, then brushed them off. But now they hit him again and again, like a relentless heavyweight champion.

"I love her," Brant said sullenly. "Helping is what husbands do."

"I'm sure Mom would have loved it if Dad had done everything for her," Myles muttered, taking one long last look at Brant before heading back inside, the sound of music growing louder before the door shut again.

Mom was different. She knew her place was on the ranch. She was strong and capable. Not that April wasn't, but the situation wasn't even close to the same. Their mother hadn't had to start over when the boys were still young. She'd never been a single mom, jobless and homeless.

Brant sat on the concrete steps of the saloon as the entrance light above flickered. Rusty, a brown-and white retriever mixed breed, ambled out of the shadows and rolled onto his back in front of him. Brant stretched out his booted foot and gently rubbed it along the dog's shaggy belly. Rusty panted, his face a ridiculous upside-down smile as he curved his spine to grin at Brant.

"I'm being dumb, aren't I? I'm acting like Heath did and over-shadowing her life and ways of doing things with my own. And worse, now I'm acting like a jealous fool instead of letting her grow and change on her own terms, and be the woman I love."

The dog panted in agreement.

Brant sighed. "So what do I do? March in there and dance with her until she forgives me for trying too hard to make every-thing perfect for her?"

Rusty continued to smile at him.

Lacking a better plan, Brant headed inside.

April allowed Cole to waltz her across the dance floor as the second song started.

"Will you tell me someday why you stayed away for so long?" she asked.

Cole held his breath while he contemplated her question, steering them smoothly through the crowd. Quite a few people had come out for his welcome-back party, announced by a banner hanging on the wall above the band.

"Sure," he said finally. He pushed her out into a spin, and when she came back toward him, the room a blur, his eyes were caught elsewhere. As he continued to gaze over her shoulder, April took a surreptitious peek.

Jackie Moorhouse sitting alone at a small table by the saloon's front window.

April swallowed, recalling the hurt she'd felt because of their fight and harsh words. Jackie thought she was undermining herself with Brant, but April knew *Jackie* was being a big chicken.

"You should talk to her," she said casually.

Cole blinked. "Sorry?"

"You should ask Jackie to dance."

He shook his head. "We have nothing in common. We were talking at New Year's and it was nothing but awkward." His attention slipped her way once again.

"Ask her about her car," April suggested.

"It's a nice car."

"Brant got her a dog."

"Yeah? Is he going to get you one?"

She looked away, feeling hurt and rejected once again, over a dog she'd requested months ago. Sure, Dodge was at the house now, but Brant often left him at the ranch after finishing his morning chores, or took him to the clinic with him. Dodge didn't really feel like the family pet.

Did Brant not think she was capable of caring for a dog?

"We've been pretty busy," she said.

Cole frowned, his face creased in thought.

"What?"

He shook his head and readjusted his grip on her waist, his embrace comfortable and familiar. If anyone had told her five years ago that he'd vanish for so long, then reappear, only for them to be able to spend a moment like this without any vile history brewing up between them--the two of them acting civil, like friends even—she would have called them a dirty liar. Maybe time really did heal all wounds. Although she was getting the feeling that Cole hadn't quite healed all of his, and that they were more layered and complex than her own.

"Tell me," she insisted, and he continued to frown.

"It's just his thing."

"I know. He's a dog matchmaker."

"No." Cole was intent, serious. "Having been away, I see stuff differently. He gets all the women close to our family a dog. So why not you?"

Cole was watching April, and her spirits plummeted.

She scoffed, trying to hide the hurt. "He married me. I'm more than family."

Cole gave a casual shrug. "Maybe he hasn't decided whether he's going to keep you or not." He winked playfully.

Instead of laughing, April felt cold dread. He'd never found a dog for Shelley St. Martin, either. Was Cole onto something?

"Can I cut in?" Daisy-Mae asked, one hand already on Cole's shoulder.

"Of course." April stepped away from him and noted how he took in Daisy-Mae's outfit with swift interest. She was dressed in typical sexy cowgirl gear despite the cool January day. She quickly fitted herself into Cole's arms as though she'd always belonged there.

Brant had given Daisy-Mae a dog. Jackie, too.

They danced away from April, and she smoothed her hands down her jeans. She needed to get off the dance floor.

"Hey," a familiar voice said, and April spun, a smile already in place.

Brant.

He looked tired.

She longed to launch herself into his arms, but hesitated, Cole's last comment still dinging around in her head like a pinball. That and her fight with Brant over her new job. And Jackie's harsh words about how she was undermining her marriage as well as taking love for granted.

April put her hands in her pockets and asked, "Are you going to get me a dog?"

"The last thing we need right now is a new pet," he said soberly.

"Why?"

"When are either of us ever home these days? You're working two jobs."

"Kurt wants one."

She saw Brant pause slightly, as though guilt was weighing on him.

She crossed her arms, studying him. "You don't think I should have a dog."

"It's not that."

"Then you don't approve of me? You don't think of me as part of the family? You don't think I'm going to stay?"

It was like all the unspoken fears of the week poured out of her mouth.

"Not here," Brant said quietly, a muscle in his jaw flexing.

"Then where?" She didn't care if people noticed their discussion. This was important. Worth fighting for. Anywhere. Anytime. "And when?"

It was time to fight it out for real, so she could figure out what was really going on inside her husband's head.

***

APRIL FUMED, trotting alongside Brant all the way home. He wouldn't talk, simply kept up a punishing pace with his long legs.

This was not how she imagined fighting with him. Fights with Heath and Cole had been fast and furious, not leaving a dull ache that pressed down on her. It hurt fighting with Brant, and she wasn't sure how they were going to fill the holes they were making with this coldness, and leaving things hanging in the air.

"What's his truck doing here?" Brant asked, pointing a finger at Heath's dual-wheeled diesel parked in front of the house.

"He's babysitting."

"It's not babysitting when it's your kid, and it's your week to have him. It's called parenting."

"I know," April said, holding her hands out, wanting to calm him. "But one step at a time." Anything with Heath was a win right now.

"Why is he here? Why is he in *our* home? He has his own house to take Kurt to."

"He's doing us a favor."

"A favor?" Brant's voice rose. "By adhering to your legal agreement?"

"Kurt needs him in his life."

"You need to set some clear expectations and boundaries. You're *divorced*."

"I know that." But if she pushed Heath too hard, she'd end up with nothing. She needed to get him where she wanted, little by little. "Quit acting so jealous. You're being unreasonable."

"Me? *Me?*" Brant was livid. More angry than she'd ever seen him.

"Yes," she whispered.

"You act like he's doing you a favor by taking care of his son. He *hit* me only a few weeks ago. And you just let him into our home without talking to me."

"He's Kurt's dad."

"In what universe do you think I want to come home to find him sitting on my couch, drinking my beer and acting like he's doing us some grand favor by finally being a dad?"

"I didn't..." April glanced at the house, where a beam of light slipped through the front window, lighting a warped square of lawn.

"You didn't think about me, did you?"

"You've been working and busy all week! I needed a babysitter!"

"To go to Cole's party."

"Yes!"

"To dance with Cole."

"Stop it. Just stop it." This was so unlike Brant she didn't know what to do. And now she had to go inside and face Heath. Thank him for his help, while having Brant shoot daggers at her with his eyes.

The front door opened and April braced herself for whatever was about to happen next.

"A paternity test?" Heath yelled, waving papers. He was lit up under the porch light, his face red with anger. "Is that kid even mine?"

"What are you talking about?" She hurried to the front steps, eager to hush Heath before he disturbed the neighbors or woke up Kurt. He stormed down the steps, meeting her on the walk. "Were you going through my stuff?"

"These were in plain sight!" He waved the papers she'd printed out for Robyn and had left above the fridge, forgetting about them after Robyn said she no longer needed them. Heath was tall enough he would have easily seen them. And apparently jumped to the wrong conclusion about why she had them. "I'm clothing and feeding a boy who isn't even mine?"

"He's yours." April squeezed his arm, hoping to ground him so he could see rationally. "I wouldn't lie to you."

"I'm not stupid, April!" Heath yelled, waving the papers again. "You're keeping me on the hook until you know this guy's in it for the long haul." He jabbed a thumb in Brant's direction.

"Hey now," Brant said, stepping in. "Let's just all calm down and figure things out. We're going to be doing this together for a lot of years."

Heath's fist connected with Brant's jaw. He went down hard, not having the time to brace himself.

"Get out of here," April screamed at Heath, rage pouring through her. "Just get out and never come back."

Brant was back on his feet, fury in his eyes, hands clenched. He looked ready to kill someone.

"Kurt doesn't need to see you two like this," she snapped, physically shoving them apart as Brant closed in on Heath. They also didn't need to give the town a good show, and due to their raised voices, she could already see porch lights coming on across the street.

"What am I to you?" Heath asked her, his breath in her face. "A big sucker? Someone to cling to? Take a look at that boy. He's a Wylder, and you've played me for too long." He turned to Brant. "Run while you can. You're just another sucker she doesn't love."

Brant's jaw tightened, but he didn't defend her. He was watching her, his expression indecipherable.

The Wylder resemblance in Kurt was not helping her right now. His bright blue eyes were like Heath's brothers, but they were also like Cole's. His dark brown hair was like the Wylders', too, but also like hers had been as a kid.

"The papers were for Robyn. Her parents wanted to get involved, but she shut them down. Kurt is yours, Heath, but if you want a paternity test, we can have one done. I have nothing to hide."

Across the street, a curtain dropped back into place, hiding whoever had been watching the fight. The men glared at each other, then her, their trust not quite strong enough to believe her.

"I'm not paying you a red cent," Heath said, aiming his finger at her before storming off. He got into his truck and slammed the door, then let down his window. "And that is the last free babysitting you'll ever get from me."

Shaking, April turned to Brant while Heath peeled out. There was such disappointment and pain in his expression she almost cried. She wished he would pull her into his arms and tell her everything was going to be okay, that he'd fix this.

"He knows Kurt's his." She took a step closer. "And I married you because I care about you, not because of anything else."

He was silent for too long.

"Brant?"

"Maybe we rushed things."

"I know we did, but it's okay. Right?" She gave him a tentative smile, hoping to cajole him out of this dangerous mood.

He rubbed his jaw where Heath had hit him, wincing. Something changed in Brant's eyes.

"I didn't give you enough time to move on and cut ties," he murmured.

"There was nothing to move on from."

"April…" Brant paused, as though deciding what to say.

"Is this about leaving the horse with him? Because Heath will always be in my life. He's Kurt's father and I will not cut those ties."

"Did you ever think that maybe I needed that horse moved?"

"Cookies was fine. I was taking care of things."

"That maybe I don't want him in my house?"

"He was babysitting."

"It's not called babysitting!" Brant snapped. "He can be a father on his own turf. This is mine, April. My turf."

His eyes were dark in the night, the glow of the porch light not reaching far enough to reveal what he was thinking. But she could feel it. Feel it growing and building like a tidal wave.

"Brant, be reasonable. He's just feeling like…" She waved a hand, trying to find a suitable word for how lost and vulnerable Heath must be.

"Did you ever stop to think how I might feel about all of this? That maybe I needed to know your ties were severed?"

"What?"

"I bought you a house. I all but kicked Laura out of it so you could move in, because you wanted to leave Heath. Then you stayed with him. You stayed, April."

"Brant, I was giving him one last chance to try to make things right. He's Kurt's dad."

"No, because you loved him. You still love him. You had one foot stuck in that door, keeping it open. Waiting, hoping, wishing. And the worst part is that I get it. He's Kurt's dad and always will be. He's the man you loved first."

"It wasn't like that at all."

"You were always breaking up with Cole. Always coming to me for support, but you stayed with Cole. You always went back for more until you had to figure things out with Heath." Brant was shaking his head, the story he was telling himself so strong she wasn't sure how she could ever break through to him. "Now it's the same, but it's Heath instead of Cole."

"Brant. No. I married *you*." She put her arms around him. His body stilled, and she felt a flicker of hope inside her.

He ran a hand over her hair, the touch a balm to the pain and fear in her heart.

"I just needed to know you were really and truly choosing me, April." He pushed her away, letting her go once she was at arm's length. "I'm sorry I made this complicated for you."

"Wait. No! I choose you. I do!" Her eyes filled with tears, making the yard and Brant's face blurry. "It's real."

He was silent for a long moment. "Maybe everyone's right. Maybe I am rescuing you, and you just needed a fake husband."

No.

She hiccupped, her breath hitching. "Don't do this. Please. Please, Brant."

His eyes closed for a moment. "We need some time to think."

"There's nothing to think about."

He was quiet.

"Brant? Talk to me." A sob caught in her chest.

"You don't need to be rescued, and that's all I've been doing.

You need some space to get back on your feet and be independent. I'll get out of your way and stop trying to make this real for you, too."

The pain in her chest intensified as she pleaded with him. "You're not in the way. Please. Please don't pull away, because I'm trying to stand up and help you, too. I'm trying to be the right woman for you." The tears caused her voice to wobble.

"April," he said, stepping toward the street, his tone wistful, "you never had to try at that."

***

BRANT HATED TO DO THIS. He hated doing it to Kurt, hated doing it to April and hated doing it to himself. But they all needed some time and space to sort out what was real in this marriage, and what was just himself and April clinging to the proverbial dream.

He'd gone inside the house, packed a bag, held April for a long minute, then walked out the door and over to the clinic, where he'd left his truck.

It was the hardest thing he'd ever had to do.

But he knew he couldn't live with the doubts, with all those nagging thoughts that were telling him he'd been a fool once again.

With a smarting jaw and an aching heart, he stretched out in the clinic's armchair with Tadpole on his chest. Tomorrow, once Robyn moved out of his upstairs apartment, he would move back in.

He wouldn't tell a soul, just let things fade away between himself and April in hopes that would hurt Kurt less. The honeymoon had been amazing, April an intuitive lover and wife. She'd always been a great friend and companion. Together they formed a good, solid partnership. When his work got crazy, she'd make supper, even if it was his night. He'd realize he was out of clean shirts for work and go to his closet to figure something out, only to find things had been washed, dried and folded, sitting there waiting for him.

But he wanted more than that. He wanted true love. He wanted April to choose him with every inch of her heart. Not because he was the safe place to run to when yet another one of her relationships was sinking.

There was a lot to think about. A lot to sort through.

He needed space.

He needed an out-of-town conference to take him away for a few days. Unfortunately, he couldn't think of a single excuse to leave town as he kicked back and closed his eyes, knowing sleep wouldn't come.

The next morning April tried to breathe through the pain in her chest. She had messed up. Her quest for independence had led Brant to believe she was using him, and not truly in love with him. The fact that he knew her better than anyone else and still had doubts about how she felt really chewed at her heart.

"Where's Daddy Brant?" Kurt asked, pulling himself onto the chair across from her at the kitchen table.

"He's working with animals," April said, figuring it was likely true. He often went and checked on herds at the ranch as an excuse to find some quiet time to think. Over the years, she'd stumbled upon him out in the pastures several times. Usually after he'd pulled his fake-boyfriend act for someone. He would definitely be out there today, seeing as he seemed to believe their marriage was a charade.

"When will he come home?" Kurt asked.

"I don't know."

"An hour?"

"I'm not sure."

Her heart constricted, whisking away what was left of the air in her lungs, at the thought of telling Kurt that Brant had left them.

"Lunchtime?"

"I don't know." She stood.

"Suppertime?"

"Kurt, I don't know when he'll be back." There was an edge in her voice, and Kurt's face crumpled. The tears started.

"Daddy Brant left us like Daddy did?"

April blinked back emotion and pulled Kurt into a hug. "I'm sorry. I'm sorry."

"For a trip? Does he go to rodeos, too? Daddy said horses need to be fixed sometimes because they get hurt. Can Daddy Brant fix them?"

April felt a rush of relief. Her son thought Brant was following the rodeo like Heath did with his stock business, and putting his vet skills to work.

"He's… You'll still see Daddy Brant," April hedged, hoping it was true. Hoping that even if her husband was done with her, he wasn't done with the boy who loved him as family.

She released Kurt, making a decision. "Come on, we're going horseback riding. Cookies needs some exercise." And they needed some fresh air, as well as a distraction.

"I don't have a horse."

"You can ride in front of me, or because it's the weekend, maybe Betty has a horse that doesn't have a rider. Maybe you can go around the ring on a horse of your own."

She winced as Kurt ran to grab his cowboy boots. Her plan made it likely she would run into Brant, as well as his questioning family. She was doing it again. Possibly ousting a Wylder from his home turf after she'd hurt him.

"Maybe we shouldn't go horseback riding," April said, checking the weather through the kitchen window. Perfectly sunny, of course. A beautiful day to face the music with the people she considered family.

"I wanna go!" Kurt's expression was so full of hope she couldn't renege.

"Fine. We'll go. Eat your breakfast first." She set cereal, a bowl and a spoon on the table, along with milk. Knowing it was likely he'd spill something, she also set out a cloth, giving Kurt his independence, wishing Brant had allowed her more of her own.

When they walked out to her SUV half an hour later, boots and hats on, she spotted Jackie's sports car still parked out front. Her heart dropped as she realized that, given all the fighting last night, she didn't know if her friend had gotten home safely. Jackie lived just down the street from the saloon, in an apartment over one of the stores, but that was beside the point. Friends looked out for each other.

April fired off a quick text, waiting to see if bubbles appeared to show Jackie was typing back. She exhaled when they did.

Will get my car later.

No word about her being aware of April's fight with Brant. Maybe she didn't know. Maybe word hadn't traveled that far yet. Or maybe Jackie was still mad at her.

Or perhaps it wasn't all about her and her love problems.

April typed out a new message. *I'm sorry for what I said.*

She waited for bubbles to appear on her screen. Nothing.

Then finally, after she'd buckled in Kurt, she saw a message.

You were right. But so was I.

April sighed. *I know.*

And now she was into her fears so deeply she didn't know how to ever climb back out again.

As she drove to the ranch, she tried to avoid thinking about Brant. It proved to be as easy as trying not to breathe.

When she pulled up behind the stables, studiously looking away from Brant's truck parked outside the nearby equipment shed, so she wouldn't cry, Betty came out to greet them.

"Cookies is doing well. We eased him in with his first riders this week."

April busied herself releasing Kurt from his booster seat, even though he could do it himself.

"I won't be using him today, as we only have a couple kids coming in," the program manager told her. "Are you going to take Kurt for a ride?"

April nodded, adjusting her cowboy hat, as Kurt ran to climb up the fence surrounding the ring.

"Are you riding together or do you need another horse?" Betty asked. "Clover's free." Her eyes narrowed when April finally faced her, and she let out a grunt. "Need to talk to Maria? She was in her garden a little while ago, talking with Carly."

"It's fine," April said smoothly.

Betty grunted again, making it clear she knew April was lying. "Men need time," she said, as though commenting on the weather. "They don't always deal well with change." She headed back into the stables.

April followed and started saddling the horses, the smells of hay, leather and her old horse calming her.

"Okay, little man," she said, hoisting Kurt up into Clover's saddle. "Hold on like I taught you to."

"With hands and legs," he said dutifully.

"And nothing too crazy."

She mounted her own horse, and led Clover with a short rope, ensuring the animal stayed in control and close to Cookies. The two horses seemed companionable, and she relaxed her worries about one of them nipping and causing problems due to their proximity. They were both well-trained, Clover used to small children and Cookies used to Kurt.

"Remember, no loud noises or sudden moves," April reminded him.

A horse trotted up alongside them as they took an easy trail that ran under some towering oaks. April turned in her saddle, her heart lifting with hope, then falling.

It was Cole, not Brant.

He took one peek at her and said, "Oh, I know that look." He gave her a sympathetic frown from under the brim of his hat.

She felt her spine slump.

"I thought the two of you would take," he said, his voice tinged with regret. He was obviously referring to her and Brant.

She darted a furious glance at him, tipping her head in Kurt's direction.

"Thought you would take the route through the pastures, that is," Cole amended quickly.

"It's the first time out with Clover and Cookies together," April explained.

Cole nodded, understanding it was an inaugural run and she was minimizing risk. Riding through the pastures meant she'd have to dismount frequently to deal with gates, as well as herds of cattle. Too many unpredictables.

"They seem to be doing fine together," Cole said. "You're a good rider," he said to Kurt.

The boy grew taller in his saddle. "I like Clover. She likes me, too. One day I'm going to ride in rodeo like Mom and Dad did. I'm going to win belt buckles, too."

"Sounds fun." Cole lifted his jacket, revealing one of his own hard-won buckles. "Want to check and see if the creek's flooded?"

"Yeah!"

April opened her mouth to protest the idea of going through the pastures to reach Sweetheart Creek, a longer ride, but Cole said calmly, "The neighbors diverted part of the creek, so a small tributary comes through over here. It's just a trickle." He raised his voice so Kurt could hear. "Betcha we find some frogs."

"Frogs are hard to catch," Kurt complained.

"Sure are." Cole led them onto a smaller trail to the left.

There was an easy fluidness to Cole's movements today, and it tickled something in the back of April's mind.

"Where did you end up last night?" she asked, watching him. She'd left the party before him, obviously, but was curious what had happened after she'd gone home to fight with Brant and Heath.

Cole had been about to point to one of the gigantic oaks, and dropped his hand, looking at her. "What do you mean?"

The way he focused on her, with no hint of distraction, was all she needed to know.

"Did you meet someone?" she asked sweetly. She'd left him dancing with Daisy-Mae. Had something interesting happened after that?

Cole snorted and rolled his eyes, causing her to have a flash of doubt.

"Here we are at the creek," he said, sliding off his mount.

"Awesome!" Kurt called from atop Clover.

April looked around, seeing just a strip of long, green grass in a sea of dry scrub. But sure enough, there was a small trickle of water.

"That's the creek?" she asked dubiously.

"I only discovered it yesterday, while out riding." Cole squinted and scratched the back of his neck. "Levi doesn't have me doing very much around here some days."

Cole helped Kurt off Clover and he ran to the so-called creek, eager to explore. After dismounting, April hitched the horses to a nearby oak. By the time she was done, Kurt was stomping in the shallow water, exclaiming over the mud and bugs.

"What happened to *you* last night?" Cole asked.

"I'm sure whatever happened to you is much more interesting."

"Doubtful." His twitching smile was a sure tell he was holding back. Remembering where Jackie's car was parked, April wanted to ask if he'd met up with her, but she didn't dare.

"Talk to me," Cole said. "You used to go to Brant for this stuff, and I take it you can't, so try me out. See if my ears are as good as his." He chuckled. "I know they're not, but... I'm here."

April sighed. "We rushed into things." And so much had been

lost and twisted around in the process, just as Brant had feared it might be. Her eyes welled, as she admitted it was her fault. She'd done what she always did.

She looked up at the sky, blinking. She didn't want to cry in front of Kurt. Or Cole, for that matter. Or even just plain cry.

"Isn't rushing into things your specialty?"

"No," she said darkly, not wanting to admit her fault to Cole.

"Maybe that's me," he said thoughtfully.

"He got weird and possessive about Heath. He didn't want Cookies over at his house anymore--"

"You seriously left your horse with your ex-husband?" Cole had stretched out in the dry grass, hands clasped behind his head, watching the clouds. He propped himself up on one elbow to study her as she sat beside him. "Your pride and joy? The horse who's been your best friend and has made boyfriends jealous due to how much love and time you squandered on that animal?" He jerked a thumb in Cookies's direction. "I thought Heath was just poking at Brant when he brought it up during that fight at the Watering Hole."

"You make it sound unhealthy," she grumbled.

"Why didn't you take the horse when you moved out?" Cole was stretching now, his fingers grazing the toes of his cowboy boots as he sat, legs extended.

For a cowboy, he was pretty flexible. "Did you take up yoga?"

"Tried it."

"What did you think?"

"I'm not crazy about staring at my own butt, yet the stretches help a lot of the aches and pains I picked up in rodeo." He jerked his thumb at her horse again. "So? Why didn't you take Cookies with you?"

"Where would I take him?"

"Here."

"Well, I didn't. But I was working on a plan." She found herself getting flustered under Cole's scrutiny. "Then Brant marched in and took care of it."

Cole let out a ho-ho of laughter. "What were you afraid of?"

"Nothing." She shot him a dirty look.

"Mom! Check it out!" Kurt squished his hands into fists, mud oozing between his knuckles.

She sighed and smiled. Good thing Brant had bought that new washing machine. "That's fun."

"It feels so cool! Wanna try?"

"I'm good for now, thanks."

"Didn't want to ask too much?" Cole asked, referring back to April's horse-boarding issue.

She nodded.

"Or were you really just keeping a foot in the door with the ex?"

"I wasn't keeping a foot in the door!" she cried in exasperation. "Why does everyone keep saying that?"

"You've been married to Brant for a month?"

She nodded.

"Divorced for two?"

She nodded again.

He gave a thoughtful hum. "This ranch is like your home, April."

"So?"

"Look at you. You had a bad day with Brant, and you're out here. Why did Brant have to retrieve Cookies and bring him here?"

"I was going to." She didn't have words to express why she hadn't. There was no reason other than this big ball of resistance that seemed to freeze her whenever she'd thought about packing up her horse and asking for more help from the family that had always been there, no questions asked. She'd known the ranch was here for her. Just like she'd known Brant was, too.

"Brant thinks I was using him." She tipped her head upward to stop the flow of tears.

Cole had gone silent, pulling up blades of grass.

"Are you listening?"

"Yup. Sure."

"You're a horrible listener."

He grinned. "Maybe you should try talking to Brant. He's really good at listening, as well as helping everyone with their problems."

"He thinks I don't love him." Her voice wobbled dangerously. Kurt looked over and she ducked her head.

"Maybe that's exactly why you called on him when it was time to leave Heath," Cole said kindly, tipping up her hat to get a better view of her face.

"Jackie said I never need rescuing."

She felt that familiar boxed-in sensation as she recalled living with Heath on the farm. She'd been afraid to accept Brant's help, afraid to reveal to him, a man she'd always admired and adored, just how lost she was. Afraid that accepting his help would mean he'd never see her as someone on his level, someone he could love.

Thirty-one, and she'd had no resources, no plan. She had not only lacked a way to support her son, but couldn't even take care of her horse. She'd been ashamed.

Talk about needing rescue.

"Jackie was wrong. I needed help." She lowered her voice. "I needed Brant."

And then she saw it. She saw it exactly how Brant must.

That she'd used him. She'd used him like a crane to lift her out of that life, that house, that marriage. He'd set her down somewhere safe with her son. He'd offered his heart, his everything.

And she'd asked him to.

But then she'd complained that he was rescuing her, and had insisted she was fine and had the reins. She'd argued that she was working on retrieving Cookies, when in truth she'd lacked the courage to do so, just like when Brant had bought her that house when she was first primed to leave Heath. She'd lost the courage to act then, too. She'd lacked the power and self-confidence to act, but when it came to Brant and their relationship, he'd seen it as emotional indifference.

It likely hadn't helped that she'd tried to wriggle her way out of the cozy web of support he'd woven around her so she could show him she was strong and worthy of his love. She'd wanted to prove she could match him, support him up the ways he supported her. Instead, she'd rejected what he was truly offering: love.

GLANCING up from checking on the Sweet Meadows Ranch southernmost herd, Brant summoned patience as he spotted a rider coming over the ridge. Heath Thompson slipped from his horse and landed on unsteady feet. He abandoned his horse, a beautiful stallion, and began weaving his way toward him, his face red with what Brant figured was anger. He wasn't in the mood to deal with a confrontation from the intoxicated man. His jaw ached from last night's blow, but not as bad as his heart did.

"You," Heath said, pointing a finger at him.

Brant squared his shoulders and faced him as he approached. "What do you need, Heath? I'm checking herds." He reached over and latched one of the bins on the back of the ranch's off-roading four-wheeler.

"You," Heath repeated. He lunged forward, swinging his arm to deliver a right hook. Brant blocked it, then allowed his frustration and anger to lead to a punch of his own. His fist connected with Heath's jaw, sending the man staggering back in surprise.

Heath blinked twice. "You hit me."

Brant rolled the tension out of his shoulders and took a step forward. "Do you want me to do it again?"

Heath massaged his jaw, then waggled a finger at Brant. "You're not who I thought you were."

Pretty much everyone in town could say that these days.

They stared at each other for a long moment. The breeze played with their jackets, the hair that stuck out from under their hats.

"Why did you come out here?" Brant asked. "To tell me I'm a home-wrecker and to deny, once again, that you're the father of a charming little boy?"

Heath continued to stare at Brant. Finally, after much apparent internal debate, he said with a heavy sigh, "I know he's mine."

Brant didn't speak, sensing a shift occurring in the man.

"He was crying all the time."

"What do you mean?" Brant asked, that familiar protectiveness building inside him. Had something happened when he'd been taking care of Kurt last night? "Is he okay?"

"We yelled all the time. And I stayed away even when I didn't need to. She never loved me." Heath flopped onto the rack on the back of Brant's four-wheeler, his alcohol-fueled fight seeming to have fizzled out.

Brant sighed. He had a lot of chores to finish, but had a feeling the man needed to talk, and it was going to take some time.

"You and April fought a lot?" he said, figuring the sooner Heath got started on his stories, the sooner he'd leave Brant alone.

"Always." He suddenly seemed too weary to sit up straight.

"Did you love her?"

Heath contemplated the horizon, his eyes filled with pain and regret. "I reckon that was the closest to it I've ever been."

Brant zipped up the medical bag he'd set on the ground with the herd's records, and dropped it into a crate beside

Heath, sizing him up. "Then why won't you let her go in peace?"

Heath slid off the machine, fists raised again. He wobbled, and Brant figured it must have been a long ride out here on horseback. Judging by the grass stains and dirt on Heath's jeans, the man had taken a spill off the beast at least once. He was lucky he hadn't broken a leg or torn some tendons.

"What's it to you?"

"Why won't you?" Brant repeated, tipping up his chin.

"She's brave. She's the best thing that ever happened to me." Heath's shoulders slumped and Brant felt for the man. He knew what kind of hole April left behind.

"She was brave to leave me, and I didn't make it easy." He looked up again and Brant instinctively tightened his muscles, rolling his weight onto the balls of his feet so he could move quickly if need be. "It was for the best. She couldn't have done it without you."

There was something in the man's tone that caused Brant to lower his guard. Heath was letting go. Finally.

Now that it was too late for Brant.

"Thanks for being there for her," Heath said, his pained eyes begging Brant for something akin to forgiveness.

Brant sighed and shook his hand when he extended it. With a tug, Heath pulled him into a hug. "Thank you."

Brant patted him on the back, unsure what to say, or whether to expect a sucker punch.

"We didn't do anything before the divorce was final," he assured him. "I want you to know that."

Heath eased back and studied his face, judging Brant's sincerity. He gave a nod that was at first hesitant, then more sure. "I appreciate that."

"And even though things are tricky between April and me at the moment, we're still married," Brant stated. "I love her, and I would put your son's life before my own."

Heath's eyes filled. He gave a brief sniff. "You're a good man. Both April and Kurt are lucky to have you."

Brant placed a hand on Heath's shoulder. "They're lucky to have you, too."

The man backed up a step, his head swinging as he gave a derisive snort. "They're lucky to have me on the road and out of their hair so often."

"You have a lot to offer."

Heath's nostrils flared and his eyes narrowed.

"You're fun-loving and spontaneous," Brant said firmly. "I tend to be a bit too serious. I have a feeling Kurt's going to need advice from you as a teenager. He's got that same spark you and April have, and I'm not sure how to raise someone like that without squelching that fire. We're going to need you." Assuming he and April figured things out, of course.

Heath's shoulders straightened as he considered Brant's words. "Yeah. You are."

"I know a lot about animals, and so does April, but when it comes to rodeo livestock, if Kurt is interested, I'm hoping you'll be the one to set him up with the right horse. One that will keep him safe."

"Yeah. I can do that." He was nodding now, looking determined. "You know he's not too young for rodeo."

"That's right. And I'm sure he'll become interested soon. Still, I worry about safety. April does, too. But I know you'll train him and his animal well."

Heath nodded.

They both paused awkwardly for a moment, and Heath glanced over to where his stallion was grazing. Then his eyes cut back to Brant. "You know April loves you."

Brant stiffened. He wasn't up for this conversation. Not with Heath. Not now. Maybe not ever.

"Always has," he added.

"Heath, we never—"

"Just listen." The man put up a hand, suddenly looking weary beyond his years. "I don't know if she recognized it as that, but I sure did. And I was jealous as hell. Still am."

Brant considered the proclamation.

"She's an amazing woman," Heath stated.

"I know."

"I felt like I was the luckiest man on earth when she turned to me that night she broke up with Cole. I knew it wouldn't last. When I found out she was pregnant, I thought I'd hit the jackpot." Heath smiled, the flesh around his eyes crinkling. The smile faded. "But I'm not the right man for her. She needs a steady rock like you. Always has. It kills me I can't be that for her. That's why…" He let out a shaky breath before continuing. "That's why it's been so hard to let her go. Because I know she's going to be happier without me." His voice hitched. "How can a woman I love be better off without me?"

He shook his head again. "Nah, but it was never really love. Not like the real stuff. We both knew that." He stared at Brant, his face creased in thought. "You know when you want the fancy sports car, even though you know you're going to drive too fast, lose control and drive it off a cliff?" He gave a crooked smile and Brant nodded, trying to understand.

"She's meant to be with you. Fight for her. Yell if you have to."

Brant shook his head. He wasn't Heath. He wasn't going to yell at his wife to get her to love him.

"No," Heath said firmly. "Take advice from someone who was married to her for several years. If a man like you raises your voice, she's going to listen." He grabbed the front of Brant's jacket and gave a small shake, then let go. "She's scared. She doesn't know how to love. I couldn't teach her that."

He patted Brant's coat and took a step back.

"Fight for her. She's who you're supposed to be with. And she'd be lost without you."

APRIL SET DOWN her phone in frustration. She'd tried to call Brant three times since returning from her horseback ride with Kurt and Cole.

Each time she got his voice mail.

They had their wedding reception at the barn outside town tonight.

Tonight!

And they weren't even speaking to each other.

She'd forgotten all about the party until Kurt mentioned it on the ride home from the ranch. Wouldn't that have been something, if Brant showed up at the event and she stood him up?

But what if she went and her husband didn't?

Somehow, even though Brant was hurting, she couldn't see him having her go to the party without him. That thought alone made her feel a bit better about attending a celebration of their already crumpling marriage.

One she hoped to save.

Brant paused in the doorway of the converted community events barn located a few miles outside of town. Sweetheart Creek used it for fund-raisers and barn dances, potlucks, and for their celebration of the Couple of the Year.

Somehow Brant had never quite seen himself as an integral part of that celebration. Or showing up unsure whether his new bride was going to be there or not. And if she was, if she was going to speak to him.

He forced himself to smile as well-wishers shook his hand, drawing him farther into the barn.

"Thank you," he said once again, as he was offered more congratulations.

He scanned the busy room, his eyes catching on a blue dress. April. His heart pounded harder and his palms grew damp.

He still loved her. There was no denying that.

But she *had* needed rescuing, even if she'd been unable to see it. What he'd done was an act of love, but he understood how she'd felt he was preventing her independence. How could they have gotten something borne of goodwill so terribly wrong?

He strode toward her, ignoring friends and neighbors who spoke to him.

He stopped in front of his wife, and her eyes lifted to his, that adorable smattering of freckles across her nose standing out as her face paled. He barely noted the people milling about, or what song was playing through the barn's sound system. Everything but April MacFarlane faded away.

"You needed rescuing," he said gruffly.

She nodded.

"Are you listening to me?"

She nodded again.

"Well?"

"I did need rescuing." Her eyes cut to the side and her voice was quiet. "And I didn't need rescuing by just anyone, either." He could barely hear it over the background noise. Her eyes finally lifted again. "I needed you, Brant. I needed the man I love. Then and now. Always."

He exhaled, letting her admission soak in.

"I love you, Brant."

His own voice was shaky as he said, "I love you, too."

"I was scared."

He nodded to show her he was listening, even though all he wanted to do was sweep her into his arms, kiss her and take her home.

She was wearing the locket he'd given her for Christmas, and she clenched it in her hand. "I was afraid, and I didn't think about what you were facing. I just wanted to be able to stand on my own two feet again and meet you in the middle."

"I realize that now, and I'm sorry."

"You mean a lot to me and always have. I was scared."

"I was scared, too. I was feeling… stuff." He finished awkwardly, shaking his head at his sudden inability to express himself. And becoming aware of their growing audience.

"*I'm* sorry. It's my fault."

"No, it's not," he said fiercely. "We're in this together, remember? We both get to screw up."

Her smile flickered, a hint of those beloved dimples flashing and fading.

"I love you, April. Not just the fun rescue parts. All of you."

Her laugh was watery, her eyes damp. "I love you, too, Brant. Even the rescuey parts."

He took her hands in his. "I know we're doing everything backward and upside down, but I eloped because my heart belongs to you and it always has." He got down on one knee, pulling something small from his pocket. "And I hope that this ring will show you just how much I care, and how much I want to be with you. Always."

He held up a sapphire-and-diamond engagement ring, the gems sparkling under the string of lights hanging above them. "This is for you, if you will continue to have me. Not as your rescuer, but as your husband. Your partner. A man who sometimes needs you to hold me up, too."

"No." She started to cry, and he felt the room spin, the hardwood floor grinding into his kneecap. "No, Brant. You're not listening. I *want* you to rescue me. I want you and nobody else. Just you. Completely the way you are—all imperfect and rescuey—because that's how you show me you care. I get that now."

"Is that a yes?" Carmichael asked. He had been milling about, a cup of punch in his hands.

April nodded, her eyes wet. "Yes. It's a yes!"

She threw herself into Brant's arms, and he rocked backward, trying to brace them as they tumbled onto the old barn floor. The ring in his fingers went flying, but with April pulled tight against him, feeling so right and at home, he couldn't muster the attention to care. Because his wife was back in his arms, exactly where she belonged.

APRIL WAS STILL in Brant's embrace, sprawled in the middle of the old barn's dance floor. She was laughing, sobbing, unable to control herself, and couldn't seem to stop. People were cheering, reaching down to see if they needed help up.

They waved away the assistance, continuing to embrace.

"Daddy Brant, Daddy Brant," Kurt was saying, tugging on Brant's arm. April shifted, sitting up beside him.

"What's up, Kurt?" Brant asked.

"You need this," he whispered. He held out his hand, the gem-encrusted ring clutched in his fingers.

April gasped as she took it in. "You can't afford that."

"Well, I figure I might once I shove my wife out of the clinic and no longer have to pay her salary."

"What?"

"Jenny said she needs you full-time. And you were right, there was never a job for you at the clinic. I made that up. Just like I made up a job for..." He glanced around, realizing half the town was surrounding them, listening to every word they said.

"It's okay. We all know you created a job for Robyn, too," Donna Nestner said, giving him a warm smile.

"Helping us strays is what you do best," April whispered.

He grinned, leaning his forehead against hers, looking more relaxed than he had in weeks. "You were never a stray."

April shrugged, happy to be one if it meant Brant would take her in and ensure she had a good home.

Still sitting on the floor, Brant accepted the ring from Kurt, then faced April, their happy guests surrounding them. Joy sprung loose within April and she felt as though she was finally in the very place she'd always wanted to be.

"Brant Wylder, rescue me." She flung out her left hand, her bare ring finger ready and waiting.

He hesitated, eyebrows raised.

She leaned in, saying, "My heart needs rescuing, and you're the only one capable of handling that job."

He slid the ring on her finger, and as she gazed up at her loving husband, she'd never felt more certain of anything in her entire life.

BRANT COULDN'T STOP SMILING. He had his arms around his wife, and they'd been holding each other since the moment she'd accepted the ring. They were already married, but he felt as though they should be planning a wedding.

As Brant and April looked on, Kurt bounced from one group of people to another, telling everyone his parents were engaged.

Brant laughed, loving the boy's energy, and sending April out into a slow spin before pulling her back to him for a kiss.

It was all real. And all of it was his.

He hadn't even had to shout and fight, like Heath had suggested.

April looked up at Brant, her eyes bright with happiness. She clutched his jaw, bringing him closer for a kiss, but paused when he winced. She angled his face, taking in the bruise there. Her brows furrowed and she sighed, no doubt worrying that her new husband and her ex were going to end up in regular fistfights.

"Heath and I had a conversation this afternoon," he told her.

Her shoulders drooped as she gave a sigh.

"And we came to an understanding."

Now her eyes widened, her brows lifted. "You did?"

"We did. We figured out how the four of us will all fit together."

"Really?"

Brant nodded. "Good things happen."

Her worries seemed to settle, and he knew she understood that while the conversation hadn't been easy, it had been good.

"Heath's a good man," he said, reinforcing the change in the two men's relationship.

Brant finally got that kiss. It was tender and sweet and full of love. "And so are you," she whispered. "And everyone knows it."

"So you didn't ruin my reputation, after all?"

"Oh, I can still try, if you'd like?"

"No, no. I'm good. I've thrown and received more punches while with you than I have in my whole adult life."

She frowned, her pitying look a bit too amused to be truly sympathetic.

"There's that bratty MacFarlane side coming out in you again."

She laughed. "You'll get used to it."

"I hope not." He liked how it kept him on his toes. He pulled her close, wrapping his arms around her as Karen and Carly sidled up beside April to look at her ring. Soon the three were eyeing Jackie, who was flitting about the barn, laughing, chatting and being her usual bubbly self.

"She's ignoring Cole," Laura announced, slipping into the semicircle that had formed. Brant groaned. He still had one more surprise for April, and her friends were stealing her away to play matchmaker, which he knew from experience could take all evening.

He forced himself to be patient. This was married life, and he wouldn't change it for the world. Even if he still needed April for one more thing to ensure a happy ending to their night.

"We should take her to a football game," Karen announced, referring to Jackie.

"Seat them together," April agreed, leaning in, her eyes sparkling.

The sport's not in season," Carly replied, crossing her arms.

"Blind date?" Karen asked. She winced at her own suggestion.

"Some sort of setup," Carly mused.

"She needs to find true love," April said.

"We'll think of something," Laura assured them. "Start a group text."

Karen pulled out her phone to set up the secret conversation, and April gave Brant a big smile, her arm around his waist as she leaned in. "I'm so glad I don't have to worry about that stuff any longer." She began drawing them slowly away from her group of friends.

"I almost forgot," he said. "I have one more thing for you."

"You do?" He loved seeing the surprise in April's expression. "You must have had a busy day."

"You have no idea." After talking with Heath, he'd brought the man to the ranch house to sober him up, before hitching up the trailer and taking him and his horse home. After dropping them off, he'd kept driving, hitting the jewelry store, then stopping at his clinic for one more thing after cleaning himself up for the party.

"It was kind of a backup plan," he said, guiding her and Kurt toward the barn's enormous doors. "Or maybe it was Plan A. I can't remember." He was too happy to make sense, and simply pulled her hand. "It's out in the truck."

"What's in the truck?" Kurt asked, bouncing along beside them.

"It's a surprise."

"Is it a dog?"

"You leaving already?" Myles asked with a smile. He'd been manning the door, and handed April and Kurt their coats. Brant was still wearing his from when he'd arrived.

"Daddy Brant has a surprise!" Kurt said. "He and my mom are engaged!"

Brant helped April into her coat, in the process noticing a table ladened with gifts he hadn't seen earlier. He looked at April in surprise and she shrugged. "You know how Sweetheart Creek is."

"I do."

"Don't worry, Daddy Brant," Kurt said seriously, catching

Brant eyeing the table. "I can help you open them all. There are too many for two people. It'll spoil you."

"Oh? It will?"

Myles chuckled and Kurt nodded knowledgeably. The boy walked to the table and patted a square box. "I heard this one's a waffle maker. Sorry for the spoiler alert." He adjusted his small cowboy hat in a way Brant sometimes caught himself doing.

Brant whispered to April, "Maybe we can have another little surprise a few months down the line."

It took her a moment to figure out what he meant. "Only one?" she asked innocently, as they made their way through the rows of vehicles parked in the grassy area behind the barn.

"I was thinking maybe two or three?"

"Boy, that's a lot. You might have to rescue me from things such as cooking dinner and changing diapers."

"I'm pretty sure it would be my pleasure." He slipped an arm around her waist, drawing her close as they walked. "But in the meantime, I have something else to eat up your time and distract you. Are you ready?"

He thought about covering her eyes, but Kurt was already pulling himself up on the running board of Brant's truck, clinging to the side mirror as he peeked through the window.

A pale brown furry face looked out at him.

Kurt lost his grip on the mirror as the dog barked, causing the boy to slide to the ground. He laughed. "It's a puppy!"

"It is," Brant said. "And it belongs to all three of us." He said to April, "They're a lot of work, but I thought… puppy. New beginnings. No old bad habits to break. Other than those me and Dodge may have picked up throughout our bachelor years, because the two of us plan on sticking around to help with this newbie."

"Hmm. Maybe I should trade you in, as that sounds a lot easier than what we've been trying to do." She winked to show she was kidding, and he planted a wet kiss on her lips.

"Don't you dare trade me in."

"I want to name it," Kurt announced.

"Go for it." He turned to April. "If that's okay with you?"

She was grinning. "You know how long I've wanted a dog? Especially one from you?"

"I'm not sure why I resisted. Maybe it was my fear of being in the friend zone."

"The friend zone?"

He shrugged. "Like maybe I'd be stuck there forever if I got you a dog. There'd be no further reason to keep me around, as you'd only want me for my pet procurement skills."

"Um-hmm." Her fingers traced their way up his thick plaid jacket, twining together at the nape of his neck, and sending a shiver down his spine. "Is that the truth?"

"I honestly don't know. But you have been hinting around for some time."

"I wanted a dog even longer than I wanted you." She kissed him.

"Is *that* true?"

"No. But now I have it all."

"Not yet," he said, his gaze drifting to her belly. "But soon. Soon."

ackie Moorhouse

JACKIE SMILED AUTOMATICALLY, her mind blank as she nodded along, pretending to listen to a gushing, happy April, who had finally released Brant long enough to socialize with a few guests at their wedding reception.

Everything was suddenly perfect for April and Brant again. Just like that.

So easy.

They'd barely been broken up for five minutes and now they were engaged, or still married, or whatever it was. They were even talking about babies.

How did everyone just fall in love and make it all happen so fast, anyway?

Although maybe things would happen for her soon, too. Jackie bit her bottom lip, telling herself not to smile, not to give anything away. Her eyes cut toward Cole Wylder. He was standing near the table of drinks in what she figured were his favorite pair of tan boots, Wranglers she recognized as new last week, and a Western button-up shirt that brought out the mountain-lake color of his eyes. He had topped the outfit with a black cowboy hat that gave him a hint of that wild something she'd had a taste of after his welcome back party, and had been daydreaming about ever since.

Forget the awkwardness that had surrounded them since his arrival. That was now gone. But it had been replaced with something even worse—a longing and feeling of missed timing.

As though sensing her thoughts, Cole's gaze scanned the partygoers. His eyes cut to hers and a warmth filled her with yearning. He gave a brief nod and turned away. Violet Granger came up beside him, looped her arm through his and leaned toward him to whisper something in his ear.

Jackie's heart stopped.

She and Cole had kissed after his party when he'd walked her home last night, but Jackie had turned down anything further. She wasn't doing one-night whatevers anymore, and he'd told her he'd sworn off women until summer, so he could focus on reconnecting with his family. That had made the whole night a nonstarter for both of them.

So what was Cole doing letting Violet flirt with him? Because that was what she was doing, laughing, trailing a finger down his biceps.

Surely Cole was still thinking about Jackie, like she was still thinking about him? There'd been a connection between them that had surely meant something.

Maybe she'd made a mistake. Maybe she should have taken whatever she could get.

Her heart sank. She didn't want anyone's leftover scraps of love any longer. She was thirty-two. It was time to ask for more than some quick, fun fling, and start searching for something real, like her friends were finding.

She sighed, feeling dejected as Violet laughed at something Cole said, showing too many teeth and trying way too hard. She liked Violet, but she was the one who'd been waiting for Cole to return. Return to her.

Cole's head turned, his eyes locking on Jackie's for a brief second that felt like an eternity. The skin near his eyes wrinkled and a hint of a smile sent a flurry of heat through her body. He gave her a slow nod before gently sliding his arm out of Violet's grip and saying something to her that made the woman frown.

Maybe Jackie didn't need to search. Maybe the beginning of what she was looking for was already right in front of her, and all she had to do was be patient for just a little longer.

And let Cole Wylder know that when he was ready to date again, she was the very first woman in line.

THE COWBOY'S OF SWEETHEART CREEK, TEXAS

Read them all!

The Cowboy's Stolen Heart (Levi)

The Cowboy's Secret Wish (Myles)

The Cowboy's Second Chance (Ryan)

The Cowboy's Sweet Elopement (Brant)

The Cowboy's Surprise Return (Cole)

There are more Sweetheart Creek stories set in Indigo Bay! Maria has her own special story, Sweet Joymaker. Their cousin Nick's story is Sweet Troublemaker. And you can't forget about the Wylders' cousin Alexa! Her story is Sweet Holiday Surprise.

<u>Indigo Bay</u>

Sweet romances set in a beach town—meet characters new and old in this spinoff series.

Sweet Matchmaker (Ginger and Logan)

Sweet Holiday Surprise (Cash & Alexa)

Sweet Forgiveness (Ashton & Zoe)

Sweet Troublemaker (Nick & Polly)

Sweet Joymaker (Maria & Clint)

ABOUT THE AUTHOR

Jean Oram is a *New York Times* and *USA Today* bestselling romance author. Inspiration for her small town series came from her own upbringing on the Canadian prairies. Although, so far, none of her characters have grown up in an old schoolhouse or worked on a bee farm. Jean still lives on the prairie with her husband, two kids, and big shaggy dog where she can be found out playing in the snow or hiking.

Become an Official Fan:
www.facebook.com/groups/jeanoramfans
Newsletter: www.jeanoram.com/FREEBOOK
Twitter: www.twitter.com/jeanoram
Instagram: www.instagram.com/author_jeanoram
Facebook: www.facebook.com/JeanOramAuthor
Website & blog: www.jeanoram.com